MARK H. NEWHOUSE

The Case of the Killer Knights

Newhouse Creative Group

First published by AimHi Press 2020

Names: Newhouse, Mark. | Traynor, Daniel, Cover

Title: The Case of the Killer Knights / by Mark H. Newhouse

Description: Orlando, FL :AimHi Press, 2020. | Summary: In the 4th book of the Monstrovia series, Brodie, Emily, and Doofinch the Defender face incredible danger as they try to unravel what caused a terrible accident that could put their friend in jail.

Identifiers: Library of Congress Control Number:2020935426 (print) | ISBN 978-1-945493-24-9 (paperback)

Subjects: CYAC: Law. | Mystery. | Fantasy. | Medieval. | Knights. Classification: LCC PZ7.N49 Cas 2020(print) LC record available at https://lccn.loc.gov/2020935426

First edition

ISBN: 978-1-945493-24-9

This book was professionally typeset on Reedsy. Find out more at reedsy.com

CRASH!!!

T he sound echoed in his head like a cymbal. He could barely see. An ugly lump formed over his right eye. Smoke streamed into the air around him. Is that coming from me, he thought.

"You crashed into me!" A voice screeched. "I should kill you right now! Your kind deserves to die!"

The sight of a giant sword, bright sunshine glinting off the sharp blade, blinded him. He staggered backward. *Who is this madman waving a sword at me? Why can't I stand?* He tried to flap his wings, but a sharp pain stopped him.

The sun reflected off the man's armor. "I hate dragons! You're all monsters!"

The dragon's eyes were clearing. He saw the raised sword and recognized the clanking sound of armor. "Dragonslayer!" Terror shot through his brain. "He's going to kill me!"

"Get out of here, filthy beast," the man shouted and dropped to the ground with a clank.

The dragon believed the man was dead. It's my fault, he thought. He heard sirens blaring in the distance.

"They're coming for you," the man raised his head and taunted.

The sound of sirens was getting louder. They were coming closer. Though terrified of the Dragonslayer, the dragon lowered his head to see if he could do anything to help. *He's breathing. "Sir, do you need help?* He wished the man could understand he wanted to assist him, but the man was waving him away with his arm.

"I said, get out of here!" The man threw a heavy metal glove at the dragon's face.

The sirens were louder.

The dragon shivered and stared at the road. *They hate dragons.* Terrified, the man still screaming at him, the sirens deafening, he stumbled to the railing at the edge of the overpass. Anything was better than facing a mob of Dragonslayer knights.

The man closed his eyes.

Thinking the knight was really dead, the dragon climbed over the railing and threw himself into the sky. At first, weakened by the crash, he dropped toward the water below. Then he forced his wings to spread wide. Though still in pain, he beat the air until he was flying. Maybe, I should go back, his mind said, but dizzy, weak, and frightened, he circled the scene and then flew off.

The knight removed his helmet. He looked up, smiled, and then closed his eyes.

The dragon knew he couldn't go far, nor fly too fast. As he scanned the sky, he saw his home, the three-story mansion of Jasper Doofinch, the lawyer for mythical monsters and fictional folk. Jasper's nephew, Brodie, would be there to help him. The boy would stop the pain. He could hear him whispering, "Horace, just come home. You'll be fine."

The sirens stopped.

A police officer sauntered over to the fallen knight. He gazed at the man's closed eyes. "Are you alright?" he asked.

"Of course, I ain't right," the knight replied, pointing his finger into the air. "Doofinch's dragon tried to kill me!"

The policemen looked up. "You got him. Good. Now close your eyes. I'll take care of everything."

The knight was happy to do just that.

CHAPTER 1

A WEEK EARLIER

My uncle, Jasper Doofinch, the lawyer for mythical monsters and fictional folk in Monstrovia, is mumbling to himself. That's always a bad sign. When he spots my look of concern, he pats down his unruly white hair and says, "Sometimes, Brodie, you have to keep a promise, even if you don't want to."

I know exactly what promise he means. I stop brushing Horace, his dragon, something that relaxes me because it takes every muscle in my body to run the big coarse wire brush up and down his massive neck. "Do you have to tell him? He may leave us."

Uncle Jasper sighs. "You're right. But I promised to win back his flying license years ago. Do you think I want him to leave? But he's like you. He stays with me because he wants to, not because I own him."

Uncle Jasper's right. I stay with him because I want to. That came as a big surprise to me. Who'd want to live with an eccentric uncle who looks like a garden gnome? It took weeks after my divorced mother sent me to spend the summer with him to appreciate that my uncle, one of the few humans in Monstrovia, is special. He's a hero. He always tries to do what he thinks is right. He always keeps his word, even if it hurts him. Like now. "Horace won't leave. He loves you. I do too." I whisper the last part. It's still hard to say.

"Thank you, Brodie. I know how difficult it is for you to say that after your parents' divorce. It took me time to realize I love you too." He sighs. "But Horace is not a teenage boy, who is now my brilliant assistant. He's a dragon, who has dreamed of being allowed to fly again for many years."

"It wasn't fair that the government took away his license like that."

"The Department of Aviation said he was too old to fly." Uncle Jasper shakes his head. "Some people think once you reach a certain age, you can't do things." He grunts. "That's called 'age discrimination.' All I did was prove that not only can Horace still fly, but he used that ability to save our lives." He scowled at me. "Some of us, my mischievous nephew, far too many times."

I get it. Being thirteen years old, I never cared about how old people are told they can't do things, like drive a car, keep a job they enjoy, or play sports, just because of their age. Being Uncle Jasper's assistant, helping him prepare for court, to fight for Horace's flying license, I discovered a lot of contributions older people made to science, art, music, and more. I was really proud when Uncle Jasper presented examples I found for him of people who continued to make a real difference at all ages. Even in their nineties and over one hundred. He looked like a hero, standing before the judge and stating, "We all get older. So, what right do we have to limit what someone can do as long as they aren't a danger to themselves or to others?"

Everyone applauded. But I didn't think that getting Horace back his flying license would mean that he might leave us.

"I worry about Horace," Uncle Jasper mutters, yanking on his red suspenders, which he needs to keep his pants up. "What if he really is too old to fly?"

"You said age shouldn't stop anyone from doing things. Don't you believe that?"

"I do believe that. But that doesn't stop me from worrying about someone I care about." He yanks on his suspenders again. "Horace deserves his license. But I'll miss him. I know he's just an old fire-breather, and they do stink up a garage..."

"I'll miss him too." I was so afraid of the giant dragon the first time I saw him, but he'd become my friend. I'm not sure how much he understands about the things I tell him, secret thoughts I never tell anyone. Not even my uncle. "Maybe he won't leave?"

"A dragon belongs in the wild with the few of his species not killed off by the Dragonslayers."

"But he loves us. Doesn't he?" I remember the night I slept in the forest, huddled to his chest, so I wouldn't freeze. He looked as if he understood he was protecting me.

"I'm sure he does love us," Uncle Jasper replies. "But that may not be enough. Horace is more than a hundred years old, but that's young for a dragon. He might want to start a family with someone he can love…someone who will love him back."

"I guess. I never thought I could love a dragon."

"I never thought you could either." Uncle Jasper puts his hands on my shoulders. "When you truly love someone, you want what's best for them. Someday, I know, you'll leave me—"

"I'll never leave you!" I wouldn't have said that a year ago. When he met me at the door of his strange mansion with a gigundo sword aimed at my nose, I was ready to race home to Brooklyn. It shows how you can't judge a book by its cover, as Mom always says.

Uncle Jasper smiles. "Thank you. But we both have to face that someday you'll want to go to college, hopefully, law school…and eventually get married." He shivers and then chuckles. "Let's not think that far ahead."

"I'll never get married."

"Not even to Emily?" When he sees the expression on my face, he adds, "Just teasing. Although Emily Beanstalk is special—"

"Never ever!" Now, I shiver. Emily Beanstalk, who I met in our first case together, is brave and smart, but boy, is she stubborn! And she can be annoying like you wouldn't believe! "Marry Emily? Never in a million, gazillion years!"

Uncle Jasper laughs. "Anyway, if Horace wants to leave, we have to accept it."

I know he's right. I stroke Horace's face. This might be the last time.

"Come with me, old friend," Uncle Jasper coaxes and leads Horace out of the garage into the sunlight. "I have a wonderful surprise for you." He unrolls the parchment license and holds it up before Horace's eyes. "It's your flying license. We won the case. I kept my promise."

Horace tilts his head. He flicks his tongue and licks the parchment.

Uncle Jasper rolls the license back up and tucks it into the collar around Horace's neck. "You're free, my friend." He strokes the dragon's neck and backs away. "You've waited for this for a long time. You're free! Now go!"

Horace peers up at the sky, then back down at my uncle.

I'm hopeful. He didn't move.

Uncle Jasper points his hand to the sky. "You're free. You can go anywhere you want, be with whoever you wish."

Horace looks back up at the endless blue of the sky. A large tear falls from his green eyes.

"You don't have to leave us," I say, missing the feel of Horace's cold nose in my hand.

Horace licks my face with his tongue. So gently, it feels like a feather.

Uncle Jasper shakes his head. "Brodie, step away. It's time."

I cling to Horace's neck and then release my grip. I wish I didn't have to and back away.

Horace lets out a low keening sound and walks toward the road. He casts a look back at us as if he knows he's saying good-bye.

Please, don't go?

The earth shakes. Horace runs. He unfurls his wings, and in seconds, my friend is soaring in the air.

Please, don't go? I beg silently again and again.

Horace swoops down over us.

He's not going.

But then, he's gone.

The sky is empty. It is so quiet. I keep hoping Horace will come back. I'll run up to him and give him the biggest hug.

But he doesn't return.

I stare at the sky. No sign of my friend. "Do you think he'll come back someday?" I finally manage to ask.

Uncle Jasper smiles. "You did."

CHAPTER 2

BACK TO THE PRESENT
I 'm sitting on a wood stool in the garage, Horace's brush in my hand. "I can't believe I miss brushing down a dragon," I say to Silas Bumbernickle, my uncle's driver, handy-man, and my friend.

The little guy twists his green mustache. "Fer a dragon, he was a pretty good fella." He chuckles. "Makes me think I'll be missin' me missus, ole Mavis, when she goes to visit her sister next month."

A shrill shout makes me jump. "Silas Bumbernickle, where be ye hidin', ye worthless loafer, ye?"

Silas jumps up as if shot. "Maybe not. Comin' me darlin'." He looks at me and laughs, "Ye'll see what it's like when that Miss Emily gets ye in her clutches, off and married—"

"How many times do I have to tell you and everyone around here that Emily Beanstalk is not my girlfriend, and never will be my girlfriend!" I throw the brush on the ground, and it bounces against the wall.

"Ye see, ye ain't even married, and she has ye losin' yer temper." Silas erupts into laughter again.

"Silas!" That loud cry is unmistakable, Mavis.

"I best be goin'. Once me sweetie starts yellin' like that, no tellin' what she'll do next." He winks at me. "But, I do loves her." He scrambles on his short legs out of the barn, leaving me staring at the spot where Horace slept along the far wall. I can see the shape of his massive body in the crushed hay that was his bed.

A shadow rises on the wall. A chill shoots through me. You can never tell what kind of dangerous creature is lurking in Monstrovia. I hope whatever's casting such a mountainous black shadow won't notice me. As Uncle Jasper says, I wouldn't be more than a snack for most of the creatures here." My best defense is to stay calm and not move, not breathe, not faint. I smell blood. The smell is unmistakable, but so is the scent of a …dragon?

I can't believe my eyes. "Horace? You've come home!"

Horace is behind the door, peering outside. He turns toward me, lowers his head, and pushes his nose into my hand.

I rub his snout gently. Then, still not believing he's back, I reach for his thick neck and give him a big hug.

A drop of water splatters on my head. When I look up, Horace has tears in his eyes. I hold him even tighter. If anyone ever told me I'd be hugging a dragon, I'd have said they're nuts, but I don't want to let go because he might leave again. When I do drop my arms, I still smell blood.

Stepping back, I see a gash in his chest, and his left eye has a large black and blue lump over it. "What happened, Horace?" I reach to examine the gash, but he pulls away. "It's okay, I'm not going to hurt you." I reach up again. Horace raises his head and steps away from me. He's never done that before when I try to touch him. "Are you hurt, boy?"

He doesn't answer. I'm not sure, even after a year here, how much Horace understands English. Dragons aren't known for being great talkers, (although the Serpentake, a client in an earlier case, spoke broken English and never shut up. It was one of the things that made him a special kind of dragon.) "Horace, were you in a fight?" I spot that he's limping toward his bed.

He drops into the hay and closes his eyes.

"Are you asleep?" I approach, and the smell of blood is strong. I need help. Uncle Jasper will know what to do.

I'm about to leave the garage when I hear a noise outside the doors. It sounds like the clanking of armor.

CHAPTER 3

Horace's snoring shakes the walls. I don't hear the clanking anymore, so I'm just sitting and watching my large friend, afraid to move and wake him. I wish he told me what happened to him.

Suddenly, a hand yanks me to my feet. It's holding me so I can't shout and get Horace to help me. I kick, punch and wriggle, but I can't break loose. Kidnappers? Someone seeking revenge on my uncle? I kick and wriggle as hard as I can with my feet off the ground, and my arms held back.

"Stop it, lad, we're protecting you," a voice hisses, as I'm dragged to the far side of the garage, still kicking and trying to warn Horace. Fear shoots through me as I see a half-dozen knights inching toward my sleeping friend. *Are they Dragonslayers? Is that what happened to him?* I twist and kick harder, and finally, break free. "Horace!" I get out one shout when the hand clamps down on me again.

"Lad, stop it now. Ye'll be alright." The knight holding my mouth shut orders.

I'm not alright. The other knights, long spears in their armored fists, are surrounding Horace. *Are they going to kill him? Uncle Jasper!* I can't scream. I can't do anything to help! I clench my eyes shut and focus all my thoughts on waking Horace.

A man in a green tunic and red cape is holding a sword a few feet from Horace's face. He raises the shining blade into the air. The sunlight from the open door bounces off the sword, and the brilliant flash of light hits Horace's good eye.

My heart is pounding.

Horace's eye opens.

Get up! Escape!

Horace leaps to his haunches, and the startled knights jump back.

"Run! Run!" I scream.

The knights are too close. Horace is backed into a corner, smoke building up in his mouth.

The man in the cape advances with his sword raised. "Dragon, you are under arrest!" He signals a knight behind him holding a thick chain.

Under arrest? They're not going to kill him? I stop kicking but look for a chance to break free.

The knight with the chain walks closer to Horace. He looks nervous, his hands shaking.

"We're not here to kill you," the caped guy says in a softer voice. "We just need to take you in with us."

Horace doesn't understand. He rears back, and the smoke in his mouth is black, laced with tiny flames.

"Let me go? I'll calm him down," I try to say, but the knight is still holding me. If Horace shoots fire at these knights, I'm afraid they'll hurt him, maybe kill him.

Horace lets out a terrible roar. Smoke is streaming from his nostrils.

The man in the cape shouts again. "Dragon, we are the law! We're here to arrest you. Surrender now, and you won't be hurt."

Horace still doesn't understand. He's building up a head full of steam and fire. In seconds the knights will have no choice. It will be him or them, and I can't do anything to stop it. I hate knights. All they ever want to do is kill dragons. In one case after another, I've witnessed their cruelty. Horace hates them too. He even tried to pull down the statue of the Dragonslayer that's outside the Monstrovia Courthouse. He's going to unleash that fireball, and they're going to kill him.

The caped man shakes his head. "Get ready. We have no choice."

The other knights aim their lances at Horace's body. He's surrounded, but I know he'll fight them until he dies. The blood I smelled earlier tells me he's already fought them. I don't want to see this.

10

The caped man is in the line of fire, sword raised, ready to give the command, but instead, orders, "The boy, let him go. Maybe he can talk some sense into the beast."

The hand releases me. I fall to the ground, coughing. I jump up, ready to kick this knight if he grabs me again. My fists are tight. That armor is going to hurt my foot, but I'm ready to kick the heck out of him if he tries to grab me.

The man in the cape says, "Boy, can you calm this beast down? We don't want to hurt him."

Horace looks ready to blow. I honestly don't know if I can calm him down. I've seen dragon rage before. Once you get them this angry, this frightened, they focus all their energy on self-defense, on building up their fire. "Why should I believe you? You're Dragonslayers."

The guy looks at me again. "Son, there's no time to argue. We're the law. I give you my word, I don't want to hurt him, but if he fires at us, my men will kill him. Now, can you help us?"

I'm free. I can run to Uncle Jasper and get him here to stop this. I can't. If I leave, and Horace shoots that fireball, he'll be toast. I walk toward the leader's position. I feel the heat as I get closer. The flame in Horace's mouth is red. There's no time to lose. I run toward Horace, and his head shoots toward me, eyes bright red, mouth opening, the ball of red and orange fire is aimed right at me. He's so mad he doesn't recognize me. He won't be toast. I'll be!

CHAPTER 4

Someone screams, "He's going to shoot!"

Their spears are about to be launched. Horace will be cut to shreds, but not before I'm bar-b-qued Brodie! "Horace! Horace! Stop! It's me! Brodie!" I inch toward him cautiously, very slowly, trying not to frighten him any more than he is. "Horace! It's me! Your friend!" I wave my arms and force a smile. Not easy to do with dragon-fire about to blast you.

"Attack! He's going to fire!" A knight shouts, his spear shaking, eager to be launched to taste dragon flesh.

"Hold your fire, men!"

The guy with the sword and cape is really trying to hold them back? I can't believe it. "Horace, they don't want to hurt you. I won't let them." I'm smiling and smiling until it hurts. The heat is unbearable. I'm staring at the biggest ball of fire I've ever seen, bigger than the ones the Serpentake shot at me. "Horace! Please, stop? Please?" I'm a few feet from his face. "Horace, it's me." I reach up, afraid to touch him. He looks demonic, flame raging inside him, smoke pouring from his nostrils...he's holding it in, still hasn't fired. "Horace? Horace?"

Horace's eyes look softer. He lets out a pitiful cry, and his head lowers.

"It's working," I shout. "He sees me. He knows me."

"He's going to fire," a knight screams. "Kill him before he kills us!"

"I said, hold your spears," the man with the sword commands.

Horace is looking right at me. I still see the flaming lava ball in his mouth. "He has to get rid of the fireball. Please, don't hurt him?"

"He's going to cook us," a high-voiced knight screeches.

12

Several knights run zig-zags in their clunky armor, lances aimed. Others cower against the walls. One yells, "He's gonna burn our butts like that other one did the last time!"

The one with the sword, the commander, shouts back at me, "Boy, if he strikes one of us, we'll have no choice. Do you understand?"

I nod. "Horace, please, don't hit them? They're not going to hurt you."

Horace still looks angry, but now looks like someone who has a mouthful of horrible food and is searching for someplace to spit it out. He lets out a loud roar, rears his head back, and the fireball comes shooting out of his mouth. The caped guy grabs me and protects me on the ground with his body as the fireball passes overhead.

The fireball lands with a loud explosion in the dirt near the garage wall.

I turn to the circle of knights. They're about to hurl their spears. Their arms are shaking at the strength they need to hold back their weapons. Their helmets are closed so I can't see their eyes, but I imagine them full of hate and fury.

"He's safe!" I shout, sweat from the fireball's heat dripping off my hair. "He won't hurt you. He's fine now. Please, don't hurt him?"

The leader stands. "Lower your weapons, men."

A few knights lower their spears, but most look poised to fight.

"I said, lower your weapons now!" The leader lowers his sword. "Thank you, boy. You saved his life."

"You really didn't want to kill him? For real?"

The leader smiles. "Some of my comrades would want to do so, but I'm the law. I only use force if I must, as a last resort."

I still don't believe him, but Horace is calming, and that's hopeful. "You keep saying you're the law. Has Horace done something wrong?"

"I'm afraid so. My men and I must bring him in to stand trial." The leader hands me a rolled sheet of paper. "This is the warrant for his arrest."

Horace is leaning against the wall. His face looks more sad than angry, eyes watching me, ready to protect me if someone makes a wrong move.

I slide the ribbon off the warrant. "I don't understand Monsterlish."

The leader sighs. "Very well. The dragon is wanted for hit and run—"

"What? I've never heard of a dragon being charged with that."

The leader retrieves the warrant. "Apparently, he caused a serious accident and left before help arrived."

"Horace?"

At his name, Horace's head shoots up.

"It's alright, boy. Nobody is going to hurt you." I turn back to the leader. "You're not going to hurt him, are you?"

The leader, sweat beading on his face, shakes his head. "If you help me, I promise none of my men will do anything to hurt your dragon."

I stare hard into the leader's face. His eyes never waver. I don't know why, but I trust him. "You have to promise he'll be safe. Promise?"

The leader holds up his sword, hilt up. "As Robin of Locksley, Sheriff of Monstrovia, I give you my word."

Why does his name sound familiar?

CHAPTER 5

I'm trying to figure out how I know this caped guy's name when out of the corner of my eye, I see movement. "No!"

Robin turns, his sword raising. "I said, lower your weapons!"

A knight in a closed helmet is about to strike Horace with his lance aimed at the dragon's butt.

Robin leaps past me, and his sword strikes the lance and deflects it from its target.

"What are you doing?" The other knight screams, pulling his sword from its scabbard at his side. "It's a dragon! It's a vicious beast that must be destroyed!"

"I said, hold!" Robin shouts as I shield Horace with my body.

The knight screams, "This dragon almost killed one of us, and you defend him?" He holds his sword in front of him. "I ask all of you, shall we permit this hideous creature to live and kill more of our brave brothers?"

A few knights circle Horace, lances ready.

"I said, put down your weapons or answer to me," Robin says, his sword inches from the other knight's sword.

"He's not hurting anyone," I plead, wishing Uncle Jasper, or Silas, will rush through the door and end this.

"I say, kill the beast now!" The knight lunges toward Horace. I hear a loud clang as Robin's sword slams against the other's weapon.

"I'll kill you, you dragon-lover!" The knight whirls on Robin.

Robin throws off his cape. He has no armor. Is he really going to fight this knight to save Horace? I can't believe that. But then I hear the clang of the swords again.

15

Robin and the knight are now fighting furiously, swords clanging loudly against each other, faster and faster as I watch in fear. "Clang, clang, clang!" The swords smash against each other, as the two continue their battle.

I feel heat building up above me. "No, Horace, no!" I rub his flank, trying to keep him calm. All he has to do is fire up his breath, and the knights will attack. They're waiting for an excuse. They live to kill.

"Hold!" Robin shouts again, as he parries blow after blow of the other knight's blade. "I don't want to hurt you!"

"That dragon is more of value than your brothers?" The other knight roars. "Then you're not fit to be one of us!"

"The law! I uphold the law!" Robin shouts as he is backed toward the wall, parrying blows without launching an attack.

"You are old and weak," the other knight taunts. "It is time for us to end the threat of these beasts once and for all!" He lunges at Robin's chest, but misses, and staggers off-balance.

Robin, unlike the others, isn't wearing armor, so one hit from the sword, and he'll be chop liver. How can he win without armor, I'm thinking, as the clanking of the swords and the shouting of the men sends beads of sweat down my face. I don't know Robin, but of the two fighters, he seems the lesser of two evils. But can he win?

Clang! Clang! Clang! The swords keep smashing against each other as the two knights lunge and dodge blow after blow. Robin is like a dancer, light on his feet and able to move with dexterity. The other knight, who the men call Baldric, is having difficulty handling the weight of the steel suit, the chain mail, and the klutzy helmet. But he refuses to stop fighting.

"Enough! I order you to cease or face the law!" Robin launches himself forward like a green missile, aiming low, striking the other knight in the back of his leg. "I do not want to hurt you," he shouts. "Hold now!"

The knight lets out a loud yelp, and his leg buckles under him. He teeters sideways and then falls to the ground making a noise like the crash of a bunch of metal garbage cans.

Robin is above him like a shot, sword pointed inches from the man's throat. "Yield now, Sir, and I shall spare you."

16

The knight croaks, "I yield. I yield."

Robin's sword doesn't budge. He glares at the man below him. "When I release you, you will leave this place and promise never to question my command again. Do you understand?" He presses the tip of the blade against the man's throat. "Nod your head if you agree."

The knight nods his head.

"I want everyone to hear you," Robin says, poking the tip of his sword into the man's neck just a touch deeper.

"Yes. Yes. I will never question you again," the knight stammers.

"I, too, am a knight. We are here as officers of the law. You violated your first duty." Robin raises his sword tip a few inches. "The law protects everyone, including this dragon." He casts me a quick look, and then says in a low voice, "I'm going to release you now. If you raise your hand again without my permission, I will chop it off. Do you understand? Nod your head."

The knight nods.

Robin raises his sword and stands.

I watch the knight below him, terrified of a sneak attack.

Robin, still holding his sword, backs away. "You may help him up," he says to two nearby armored men.

They move forward, eyes warily on Horace. Together, they haul the fallen knight to his feet. He seems about to fall again, legs wobbly, helmet askew.

"Take him outside. Let him rest. I'll deal with him later." Robin sheaths his sword and picks up his cape. "I'm sorry about that. Some of our order do not share my love of the law." He wipes sweat from his brow.

"I thought he was going to sneak attack you when you moved your sword off his throat," I say, thinking how kids in school would have done that in a heartbeat.

Robin shakes his head. "He's a knight. Our word is golden. Once we pronounce an oath, it is a violation of our brotherhood if we don't mean it."

"So, you meant it when you said you don't want to hurt Horace?"

"I only want to bring him to jail so he can be given a fair trial." He glances at Horace. "He looks like a decent fellow, for a dragon."

"He's great," I reply. "I know he's innocent. He wouldn't hurt a fly."

17

"Only a knight?" Robin smiles. "Perhaps he is innocent of this crime, but if he doesn't go to court, think what could happen? Just as my hot-head associate tried to kill him, others might too. A trial is the best way to prove he's innocent and protect him."

I guess he's right. "Horace, I want you to go with this nice man. He won't hurt you." I pull Horace's head toward me. "Come on, boy, you know I won't let anyone hurt you." I spy the knight with chains walking toward me. "Does he need those?"

Robin nods. "I'm afraid so, son. You can make it easier, though."

I nod and take the end of the chain. "Horace, it's only for a little while." Does he understand? I don't know, but he only shivers when I pull the chain around his wings. "Grab the other end," I say to a knight who advances slowly and then grabs the end of the chain. I run over to Horace's other side, and he shoots his head toward me. "It's okay, Horace."

The knight hands me a large lock.

I look at Robin, and he sighs. "I'm sorry, but it is for his safety. If the men think he can break free, they'll protect themselves, as they should. We don't want to see him get hurt."

I clamp the lock shut, and Horace lets out a low moan.

"We need to get him to the cart," Robin says, putting on his cape. "Will you help me?"

I can't look at Horace's eyes as I lead him to the cart. It's enough I hear his moaning. I'm almost glad when the cart leaves. I hate how pitiful he sounds.

"You did the right thing, son," Robin says, dropping his arm on my shoulder.

"I hope my uncle thinks so," I reply, wishing Uncle Jasper was home. Wait until he finds out about this! On second thought, maybe I don't want him to get back too fast.

CHAPTER 6

"You said the sheriff's name was Robin of Locksley?" Uncle Jasper asks, after throwing a major fit when I gave him the news about Horace.

"Do you know him? He didn't act like other Dragonslayers we've run into. He actually fought a duel to stop another knight from hurting Horace. You should have seen it. It was like out of the movies, swords clanking, and Robin jumping all over. He didn't even have a suit of armor on and won! It was amazing! It was fantastic!"

Uncle Jasper frowns. "If you'd done more reading, you'd know that Robin of Locksley is also known as Robin Hood."

"That's why his name was familiar. Robin Hood lives here?" If I knew it was Robin Hood, I would have trusted him right away. "I thought he was an outlaw. He said he's the sheriff?"

Uncle Jasper pulls out a book from his shelf. "The Adventures of Robin Hood is one of my favorites. I admire how he robbed from the rich and gave to the poor. I was proud to defend him against Prince John. That was, of course, before the tyrant was forced to sign the Magna Carta." He eyes me sternly. "You do know about the Magna Carta? Prince John was forced to sign it by the nobles to limit his power. It is the basis of much of our law." He hands me the leather-bound book. "I devoured Locksley's adventures when I was a boy. They inspired me to help the poor as well."

"But you're a lawyer. Dad says all lawyers care about is making money."

Uncle Jasper looks disappointed. "By now, I thought you knew me better. Of course, like everybody else who works, I need to make a living. But what

19

I love most about being a lawyer is helping people."

"People?" There aren't a lot of people in Monstrovia.

"You know what I mean. A lot of times, people can't afford a lawyer, but I help them anyway. You see…"

Oh no! He's starting one of his lectures! I used to hate lawyers, mainly because of my parents' divorce, but from working with my uncle, I'm kinda' changing my mind. "So, even if Horace can't pay, you're going to help him?" I interrupt his lesson.

Uncle Jasper pulls up his suspenders. "I'm going to try. But it could be a difficult case."

"Anybody can have an accident," I say. "Mom says I'm an accident waiting to happen."

"Hmmm. I can understand that." Uncle Jasper opens a file on his desk. "Unfortunately, the Sheriff says Horace left the scene of the accident. You know that leaving the scene of an accident is called "hit-and-run." It's a serious crime. You never leave the scene of an accident. Never. Never."

"Why is it so serious? If I had an accident, I'd want to run away too." I thought of the time I shot mudballs at my principal's car with my slingshot—one of the reasons why Mom sent me to my uncle in the first place—I ran like crazy, so I wouldn't get caught. Of course, he knew I did it. They always know. Boy, did I get in trouble! It wasn't the first time nor the last, but I'm doing better. My goal is to become a lawyer someday, and Uncle Jasper says no law school will accept me if I break the law.

"I suppose it's human nature to run away after you've done something wrong. But what if you hurt someone? Wouldn't you stay to see if they're okay?" Uncle Jasper shoots me one of his "lawyer looks." He makes his eyes stare right at you as if they're digging holes in your pupils. He says it makes people want to tell the truth. It sure works on me.

I shift uneasily in my chair. "Yeah. I guess sticking around would be the right thing to do."

"Of course, it is. I know you, Brodie Adkins the Third, if you hurt someone, you would want to be sure they are okay. You're a good boy, even if you used to get in mischief in your old school. He gives me a warning look. "It's only right to be sure you haven't done serious damage and to take responsibility for your actions." He slaps the folder closed. "Yes, that's it precisely. You must take responsibility for what you've done."

"But it seems stupid to just wait around until you're caught."

"That's the whole idea of law, my boy. When a person commits a crime, they must be made to know what they've done. And, if necessary, be punished...so they don't do it again, and more importantly, so nobody gets hurt or killed."

"But you get them off. Isn't that your job?"

"I don't always get them off."

"Most of the time." He's really a great defense lawyer, which is why he's called, Doofinch the Defender.

"The way it works is that a defendant must be considered innocent unless it is proven beyond any doubt—reasonable doubt—that he, or she, did what they are accused of. That's called the 'presumption of innocence.' It is the most important idea in our system of law in the United States, of which we are a secret sector. Yes, dear nephew, you are innocent unless you are proven guilty in a fair trial."

Another lecture. "I get it. Because it protects everyone, including me, from being punished until I get a fair trial. Right? Except by Principal Feeney."

Uncle Jasper smiles. "You've learned a lot."

"So how do we get Horace off?" I'm confident he has the answers already.

Uncle Jasper looks down at the file on his desk. "I'm not sure we can. There are witnesses. They say they saw Horace crash into the victim and then fly away before the police arrived."

"Maybe, he was frightened?"

"Accidents are frightening, but that's no excuse for leaving the crash scene."

"Maybe he didn't know about a hit-and-run?"

"The driving test, which Horace had to take to get his license, clearly states that "In the event of an accident, all parties are required to remain at the scene until help arrives." Uncle Jasper closes the folder again. "No, I'm afraid there's absolutely no excuse for leaving the victim of an accident."

"Aren't you judging him without hearing his side? You always tell me we have to hear all sides before we know the whole story."

Uncle Jasper rises from his chair. He stands below the oil painting of him wearing a gold suit of armor. The massive portrait shows my uncle holding a helmet with a red plume rising from its top in one hand, and a law book in the other. He'd look like a great heroic knight, except for his stubby body and white, wispy hair. He looks at his portrait and then back at me. "You're absolutely right, and I will do everything possible to defend him. That is the oath I took to become an attorney. It is what I owe a dear friend."

"And we'll win." I give him a confident smile.

"I hope so. I sincerely hope so."

I wish he didn't sound so uncertain. I wish I didn't feel that way too.

CHAPTER 7

I still shiver whenever I see the gigundo concrete building called Giant Courthouse. It looks like it stretches clear across the sky. There are no trees to break up the fortress-like face of the windowless front wall. Some huge statues appear to be guarding the building. There is even one honoring the legendary Dragonslayer. I laughed when Uncle Jasper told me how Horace wanted to tear it down and have a statue honoring dragons erected instead. Now it doesn't seem funny. Horace is in big trouble, and only my uncle can save him.

Silas is standing by his yellow, mushroom-shaped cab. Without Horace to take us, since he is in jail, we were forced to ride with our crazy driver. He loves zipping in and out of traffic, throwing me back and forth in the hard leather seat, even with my shoulder harness on.

"I went special slow fer ye, me best friend in the whole world," he says, as I stumble out of the cab and nearly fall to the ground on my rubbery legs. He has to be the worst driver in the world.

"Thank you." I'm wondering how my Uncle is already so far ahead of me and why he isn't wobbly like I am from that awful ride. If anyone deserves to be in prison for crazy driving, it's Silas Bumbernickle. But it's Horace, our poor dragon, that is now on trial for causing a serious accident and then running away.

I run to catch up, but my uncle's already past the entryway guards.

"You! Human! Empty your pockets!" A huge bear-headed guard glares at me.

I hate these 'bear-heads,' but have learned to keep my mouth shut as I pull my pockets out to show I've nothing in them.

"Go through," the guard says.

I walk through the metal detector.

"Stop!" A guard steps in front of me. "Raise your hands and step over here."

"Oh, come on?"

"Raise your hands and step over here." Bear-head repeats in a raspy voice.

"Oh, brother! You guys are always picking on me." I stomp toward him.

"Is you showing temper?" A second guard asks, a metal club in his paw.

"No. I just don't know why you keep bothering me." I do know. These bear-heads hate humans. Most of the creatures here do...unless we're their dinner.

The first guard starts sniffing all over me with his black nose. "Sniff, sniff, sniff, sniff."

"Do you mind?" I lower my hands. "What are you looking for?"

The guard rasps, "Keep your hands up." He raises the club over my noggin.

"What are you gentlemen looking for?"

I breathe a sigh of relief.

"What are you looking for?" Uncle Jasper asks again.

"Mr. Doofinch?" The bear-head with the club asks, "Is dis boy wid you?"

"Lower your hands, Brodie." Uncle Jasper smiles at the guard. "He is my nephew. Now, why are you detaining him?"

The 'sniffer' growls, then says, "We detected a strange material on his person, Mr. Doofinch, sir."

"I see. Brodie, do you have a strange material on your person?"

I don't even know what that means. I shrug my shoulders.

"You see, gentlemen, there's nothing to worry about." Uncle Jasper places his hand on my back and nudges me forward.

"But Mr. Doofinch, sir—"

"Thank you for doing your job so well," Uncle Jasper says, and pushes me along. "Now, Brodie, what do you have that set off the alarm?"

"Nothing that I can think of."

"Stand here and empty your pockets again."

I think this is a total waste of time, but I empty my pockets again.

"What's that?" Uncle Jasper asks, reaching toward my pants pocket. "Something's shiny."

I reach down. I find a tiny folded piece of chewing gum wrapper stuck to the pocket's inner seam. "That set off the alarm?"

Uncle Jasper holds it up to the light. "There you are."

"It's smaller than a pencil eraser?"

"It shows how safe we should feel with these sensitive machines and conscientious guards." Uncle Jasper throws my gum wrapper into the trash. "No more gum, young man." He laughs. "And no more giving these officers a hard time. They're only doing their duty."

"Don't you think it's an invasion of privacy?" I ask, putting my pockets back in place. "I mean, you can't even have a tiny gum wrapper in your pocket without them knowing about it."

Uncle Jasper stops walking. "I think that's a good question for you to consider; the issue of how much privacy we must be willing to give up in exchange for safety. We'll make that a research project. But for now, let's focus on Horace. That is why we're here."

"If Horace is found guilty of leaving the accident, what kind of punishment will he get?"

"I'd rather not think about that. Let's just make sure our friend isn't found guilty."

"So, you have a plan?" We're in the courtroom and walking through the empty gallery toward the defense table in front of a highly-polished wood railing.

"I think so," Uncle Jasper says, pushing the swinging gate forward.

"I hope," I reply, pulling out my yellow legal pad and waiting for the judge to enter.

"Good morning, Brodie."

"Oh, no. Not again?" I sag into my chair. I recognize the voice.

CHAPTER 8

"Good morning, Emily," Uncle Jasper says, as Emily Beanstalk sits down, next to me.

"What's she doing here?" I hiss to my uncle.

"Be nice, Brodie. Horace needs all the help we can give him. I've asked Emily to assist us."

Emily gives me her sugar-sweetest smile. "I'm glad to see you," she whispers, still smiling.

I nod. As much as Emily drives me nuts, she also gives me a funny feeling. She's smart, brave, and as stubborn as Mom, but she's not my girlfriend! I repeat, Emily Beanstalk, born Bordenschlocker, is not my girlfriend! "It's nice to see you too," I mutter, wondering why I said that. I turn back to my pad and write down the name of the case: *Monstrovia vs. Horace the Dragon.* Out of a corner of my eye, I see Emily pulling papers from her briefcase. I'm surprised she isn't wearing her fancy gold, clothing, but is neatly dressed in a gray jacket and pants. My uncle scolded her in our first case when she showed up in court, looking like a movie star. He explained that juries don't like flashy clothes and lots of jewelry. I guess Emily finally understands that. Even her hair looks okay, and no diamond tiara.

Emily smiles at me again.

Darn! She caught me looking. I turn away, but I'm glad I'm wearing my best suit. I hide my sneakers under the table. It's almost impossible to find shoes for humans in Monstrovia.

The courtroom is filling up. Pixie photographers are flying around the back, bulbs flashing. I wonder what celebrity is grabbing their attention. "Oh, no!"

In walks Hugh B Goode, a giant lawyer who bears a remarkable resemblance to the posters I have of Perry Mason, a television lawyer my uncle admires. He's tall, broad-shouldered, with jet-black straight hair, and dark, powerful, eyes. I hear his husky laughter all the way in the front of the room as the pixie photographer flashbulbs "pop, pop, pop!"

Goode slithers over to our table and flashes his best Hollywood grin. "Well, well! If it isn't Doofinch and his nephew? Dudley…Dooley…er…Dilly?"

"Brodie," I correct him before he says something worse. "It's Brodie Adkins."

"Ah, yes, Brady. How nice to see you again, child."

Child? I hate this slimy character.

"And is this the charming Miss Beanstalk again? How is that lovely mother of yours? I haven't seen you, nor your mother since Doofinch tricked the court into freeing your murderous brother. Has he killed any kind old ladies lately?"

Emily is about to let him have it but stays quiet.

Uncle Jasper's hands grip the edge of the table, but he sounds calm and friendly when he replies, "It's good to see you, Goode. After our last courtroom encounter, I'd heard you were in a rest home."

Goode leans over our table. "That was a fluke, my friend. I underestimated you and your 'high-priced' legal team." He sneers at Emily and me. "Trust me, Doofinch, that won't happen again." He bares his perfectly white, picket-fence teeth. "Your dragon is going to prison for a very long time, and there is nothing you can do to stop it." He pulls himself up to his full height. "Enjoy your day. I know I will."

I'm angry and frightened, but my uncle says, "You know my friend is innocent."

Goode laughs. "That's what they all say." He winks at Emily.

I'd like to punch him. How can Uncle Jasper stay so calm? He's still smiling at this weasel?

Goode flashes his teeth again. "It's a pleasure seeing you again, Miss Beanstalk. Please give my regards to your lovely mother…and accept my condolences on taking part in this 'loser' of a case."

Emily looks like a teapot about to boil over but smiles. My uncle taught her well.

Now if I'd said anything like that to her…watch out!

There is a sudden hush in the room.

Goode hurries to his table where his secretary is arranging his papers.

"Hear ye! Hear ye! Giant Court 213 is in Session. The Honorable H. P. Wolf presiding."

"H.P. Wolf?" I wince at the shadow of a wolfish face and in walks the honorable H.P. Wolf. If ever there was a wolf in a judge's clothing, he is staring at us now.

Uncle Jasper looks as if he's seen a ghost…or a wolf.

Emily's eyes are so wide they look like her swimming pool.

Me? I'm thinking about how I'll have to say good-bye to my friend, Horace. No way are we going to win this case, not with the honorable H.P. Wolf, presiding. He hates Uncle Jasper. I can see it in his narrowed eyes and bared teeth. First Goode. Now, this? What else can go wrong?

CHAPTER 9

"Is he the judge?" I whisper to my uncle while everyone gets ready for the disaster to begin.

My uncle leans toward me. "I'd heard he was made a judge, but I never thought he'd be on this case. Maybe he'll 'recuse' himself since he knows me."

"You mean since he hates you for beating him?" Both Goode and Wolf in the same trial? Not good. Not good at all.

"Recuse means excuse himself from the case," Emily whispers.

I shoot back, "I know what it means. Shhh."

Emily sits back in her chair.

Uncle Jasper gives me a sharp look. "Brodie, you should know, lawyers do not hate other lawyers for doing their jobs well," he replies but looks nervous. "I'm certain Judge Wolf doesn't hold a grudge."

"I don't know about that." To me, court trials are like contests. There are winners and losers. It's like sports. Sure, there's being a "good sport," but everyone knows that's phony. "You beat him. Do you really think Wolf liked that?"

Uncle Jasper looks at me. "I know it seems as if a trial is a game, a contest, but the real purpose of it is to find the truth."

"Sure it is," I say. "That's why you guys fight so hard?"

"Yes, it gets 'hot' sometimes, and tempers flare. But both sides, and the judge, or jury, really want the same thing; justice."

Emily says, "Justice means—"

"Emily!"

Emily sighs. "I'm just trying to help you."

"Don't help me," I growl.

Emily just shakes her head and gives my uncle one of her smiles.

I ignore her. "So, Goode doesn't really hate you?" I look around my Uncle and see Goode's eyes rush to meet mine. Definitely, not friendly.

Uncle Jasper leans closer, covering his face with a folder. "Mr. Goode is a bit different. He wants to win because he plans someday to be Governor of Monstrovia. I suspect he also wants to be the first President of the United States from Monstrovia."

"You're kidding?"

"He's very ambitious. Losing a case makes him look bad and could cost him votes."

"So, he's really not interested in helping people. Just himself?"

Uncle Jasper straightens his tie. "My boy, there is nothing wrong with having ambitions. In fact, I think you wanting to become a lawyer is a good ambition. It makes you want to do better in school and keep out of trouble. Remember, people who commit crimes can't become lawyers—"

"Yes, I know." I hope I've intercepted another lecture about how I used to get into trouble in school back in Brooklyn, one of the reasons I got sent to Monstrovia. "I still don't like that H.P. Wolf is the judge on Horace's case."

"Neither do I. But I trust the system. I'll watch Judge Wolf like a hawk. If our wolfish friend shows any sign of unfairness to our client, I'll protest."

"But aren't judges the bosses in the courtroom?"

"The real boss is the United States Constitution and laws that have been passed for hundreds of years. Nobody is above the law. Not even judges."

"I guess."

"I'm worried too," Emily whispers, leaning so close I can smell her perfume. For once, Emly and I agree. That's really scary.

CHAPTER 10

Judge Wolf, in a long black robe, sitting behind a high desk, looks down at the prosecutor's table. "Ah, Mr. Goode. Welcome to my neighborhood."

"Oh, no! Is he rhyming?" I whisper to my uncle.

He shakes his head. "This could be a long trial. It could last quite a while."

"You're rhyming too," I hiss.

"Nonsense," he shoots back at me but looks a bit upset.

"Doofinch, if my eyes don't deceive me? The last time we met, you did grieve me."

"Your honor, I remember. Wasn't that last December?" Uncle Jasper looks at me as if he realizes he's helpless to stop rhyming.

The judge's eyebrows shoot down. "Mr. Doofinch, in my court, there will be no wasting of time with rhyme. Do you hear? Is that clear?"

"But he's rhyming," I whisper to Emily.

"He's the judge," she whispers back.

"I apologize, your honor." Uncle Jasper says.

The judge nods and sees me. "I remember your nephew's face. Wasn't he the one who solved the Beanstalk case?"

"Yes, your honor. I'm very proud of him." Uncle Jasper pats my shoulder.

"And at his side, is that his bride?"

I almost shout out, "What?" but hold it back.

The judge chuckles. "Of course, a joke I've flung. For marriage, they're much too young."

The whole court bursts into laughter. Except me. I flush bright red. I have no idea how Emily reacts. I avoid looking at her. Grrr.

The judge hits his gavel again. "Now, let's get serious. A courtroom is no place to be delirious. Bring in the prisoner from his cell so his story he can tell."

"This rhyming is killing me," Uncle Jasper hisses to me.

I nod but stare at the sight of a half- dozen heavily armed knights surrounding my friend, Horace. My sad-faced friend is wrapped in leather straps and chains, dragging an over-size black ball behind him. His eyes point down at his feet as if he's ashamed.

I want to call to Horace, cheer him up, but Uncle Jasper drops his hand on my arm. All I can do is watch the guards lead him to a cage with thick black bars on all sides.

"Your honor," Uncle Jasper says, standing, "May you please remove the shackles from the defendant? He's not going anywhere. He's in a cage."

Goode springs from his seat. "Your honor, with all due respect, this defendant is extremely dangerous. It took Robin Hood and a dozen knights to arrest him. Read the Sheriff's report, sir, and you'll agree that the safety of the court must come before the comfort of a prisoner."

There's no way this judge is going to help my uncle's client. Horace is going to be stuck in jail forever.

The judge cranes his neck, studying the cage, Horace's head poking out through a hole in the roof, eyes nearly shut. "Mr. Goode, I've read the reports. Though dragons have a bad reputation and can be very dangerous, I believe Mr. Doofinch has known Horace, the defendant, for many years. Mr. Doofinch, are you willing to vouch for him at this time?"

"Yes, your honor," Uncle Jasper says. "Most definitely."

The judge says, "Guards, remove the defendant's shackles while he is in the cage."

Wow! Score one for Doofinch! Maybe this won't be so bad after all.

"Clerk, please read the charges," The judge says.

A uniformed bear-head female announces, "The accused is charged with deliberately injuring a member of the Loyal Order of Knights, and leaving the grievously wounded victim before the arrival of assistance."

The judge snorts. "Mr. Doofinch, these are serious charges indeed. How does the defendant plead?"

Uncle Jasper stands. "Not guilty of all charges, your honor."

"Very well, let's begin? Mr. Goode, you may make your opening statement."

I grab my pad and pen. The battle is about to begin. Am I rhyming too?

CHAPTER 11

The opening statement in a trial is a very important element. It spells out the arguments the lawyers are going to present. (Oh no, I'm doing it too.)

Goode approaches the podium, smiling warmly at the judge. Since this is a hearing, the verdict will be decided by the judge, not a jury. That means the opening speech is usually shorter and more direct. Uncle Jasper explained to me that jury members, even Monstrovians, can be swayed by appealing to their emotions, so lawyers tend to be more dramatic in front of juries than when they present to judges who are trained not to react to such tactics.

"Why is this case with a judge and not a jury?" I ask.

"Good question. In most cases, a jury is used for criminal trials because the Constitution protects the accused's right to be judged by his 'peers.'"

"What does that mean?"

"Peers means like normal people," Emily says. "Like me."

She's anything but normal, I think, annoyed she's showing off again.

Uncle Jasper gives Emily an approving smile. "Peers are people like you, Brodie, not trained in law." He leans closer. "Judges are trained in law. Sometimes, I'm not sure about that, though." He laughs and then looks frightened. "Wolf didn't hear that, did he?"

I shake my head. "But wouldn't it be better to be judged by someone who knows the law? That seems like common sense."

Uncle Jasper scratches his head. "You really should be a lawyer. You ask tough questions."

"I'm being taught by the best."

"Thanks a bunch!" He looks thoughtful. "Before jury trials, all cases were resolved by judges. The problem was the judges were kings or picked by the kings."

"I get it. So, the judges were working for the king."

"Pretty much. The king picked his friends and expected them to be grateful and loyal."

"And if someone got in trouble with the king, they were judged by the king's judges, so it wasn't very fair," Emily adds.

"Exactly. That's why the right to have a jury trial is so important that it's in Magna Carta and the Bill of Rights," Uncle Jasper says.

"The Bill of Rights are the first Ten Amendments to the Constitution of the United States," Emily says. "You do know about those?"

"Yes, Emily."

"I'm only asking," she says.

I ignore her. "If we have the right to a jury, then why aren't we asking for a jury trial?"

"Something the 'great lawyer' doesn't understand?" Uncle Jasper laughs but quickly becomes serious again. "We can ask for a jury because Horace is accused of a serious crime."

"Exactly. So why aren't we?"

Uncle Jasper holds up a thick book. "This book is a textbook about dragons used in our schools. Look at the pictures and tell me what you see?"

I flip through the pages. It's not long before I can guess what my uncle wants to show me. "Every picture shows dragons as ferocious monsters. Huge flames shooting out of their mouths. Smoke is curling black from their nostrils—"

Emily leans over me. That perfume again.

"And dead people all around...some badly burned." Uncle Jasper says. "Now, look for pictures of knights."

"They're cute," Emily says.

"I don't have to look. Every knight is shown as brave, fighting courageously though they are much smaller than the dragons."

Uncle Jasper frowns. "In other words, the knights are the good guys—"

"And the dragons are the bad guys." I close the book. "We were always taught that in school too, even in Brooklyn, where we thought dragons were just myths…scary monsters in fairy tales."

"Jurors are only human. Well, maybe here they're not in Monstrovia, where we are a minority. But jurors can be influenced by their prejudices and fears." Uncle Jasper looks accusingly at me.

I get the message. I've been prejudiced against the creatures I've met in Monstrovia too…even Emily, who is half-human.

Uncle Jasper smiles. "I thought with a judge, sworn to be impartial, Horace would stand a better chance at being treated fairly." He shot his eyes up at Judge Wolf. "Of course, I didn't plan on landing Judge Wolf. But even he is sworn to not let his personal feelings affect his judgment. If he does, I have the right to protest to a higher court."

Emily nods. "So, that is why you decided not to ask for a jury. Makes sense."

"That, and the fact that a trial with a judge tends to go much faster. I don't want poor Horace to stay in jail longer than absolutely necessary."

Time will tell if my uncle made the right decision. Mr. Goode, all silk and shiny, is beginning his opening statement.

"Your honor, the state will prove that the accused, Horace, did deliberately crash into Sir Lance A. Little, a brave knight."

I wrote the words 'deliberately crashed' on my pad.

"The accused defendant then left the scene of the accident without caring that his defenseless victim was seriously injured, perhaps killed. "

"He tried to kill him," a knight shouts from the last row in the gallery.

"Kill the dragon! Kill the killer!" The knights stomp on the floor with their steel shoes.

"Silence! I'll have no disruptions in my courtroom," Judge Wolf shouts as he bangs his gavel on his desk.

Goode smiles at the knights who quiet down, and continues his speech, "We have witnesses who saw the entire crime. The law makes it clear that the defendant's actions are serious crimes. The state demands that Horace is made to pay for his vicious attack and the criminal offense of leaving the scene in a hit-and-run."

"Hit-and-run," Emily starts to explain.

"I know," I hiss.

Goode continues, "Sir Little, as you shall see, is no longer capable of working, permanently paralyzed by his injuries." He walks toward his table, where a man, bandaged from head to toe, like a mummy, is held by straps in a wheelchair. "This is Sir Lance A. Little. Just look at him. Look at him!"

The whole gallery is straining to see the knight who is letting out one low moan after another from under his bandaged face.

Goode puts his hand down on the knight's shoulder, and the knight lets out a horrendous howl. "Oh, sorry. I forgot." He points his finger at the knight. "Here, my friends was once a noble and loyal knight. But look at him now. He deserves the respect of all for his career of dedicated service and bravery. He deserves justice!"

A lot of heads nod in agreement.

I'm tempted to sympathize with the injured man myself. The knight looks pitiful. Could Horace have really done this?

Goode continues, "This dragon, like all of his species, has a tendency toward violence. But far worse, he has murderous hate for the Loyal Order of Knights, a prejudice that is totally underserved by these brave servants of justice and the Monstrovian way."

"Here! Here!" yell the knights, stamping their steel boots on the wood floor.

Judge Wolf raises his gavel, and the commotion stops.

Goode casts an approving look at the rows of armored men and says, "It is this blind hatred of all knights that drove the defendant to plow into Sir Little and leave him to die. It was this irrational, wrong, hate that let him leave poor Sir Little lying in a puddle of his own blood, unable to walk, unable to call out, unable to see, until help finally arrived. Can you imagine leaving such a brave warrior to die in the gutter?"

"No! No," the knights chant.

Goode waits for silence and then continues, "What kind of monster can do such an uncaring thing?" Goode lets his eyes pass around the courtroom. "I know of only one." He raises his hand. His finger points to Horace. "Dragons."

Horace, long neck sticking out of a hole in the top of the cage, looks like he wants to bite Goode's pointing finger off.

I pray he doesn't, and thankfully he doesn't. He closes his eyes and keeps his mouth tightly shut. The finger is safe.

"Only dragons are ingrained with such hate and violence. Thank you, your honor." Goode bows his head to the judge and returns to his seat while casting glowing looks at the gallery.

"He's darn good," Emily whispers.

"Your turn, Mr. Doofinch," Judge Wolf says.

I'm always worried when Uncle Jasper makes his opening speeches. Unlike Goode, who is tall and dresses well, a blue tie with American flags a part of his courtroom attire; Uncle Jasper gives the impression of a stumpy, clumsy, bumbler when he waddles toward the podium. I hate his red suspenders and plaid jackets. He says his clothes are part of his personality, but I think he dresses this way, so opponents underestimate how smart and cool he really is. He wants other lawyers to believe he's no match for them. He fooled me too. He's like a magician pulling a rabbit out of his hat. Only his hat would be dusty, shabby-looking, and some awful color like vomit-yellow.

Uncle Jasper speaks in a softer voice than Goode, "Your Honor, Mr. Goode has forgotten the most important thing about this, or any other case: Horace is innocent unless it can be proven beyond any doubt that he **deliberately** attacked Sir Little, and **deliberately** left after the accident. We will prove there is no evidence that, if these events actually occurred…we're not saying they did…that they were **deliberate** and **planned**. If Mr. Goode can't prove that they were **deliberate** and **planned**, beyond any possible doubt, my client can't be found guilty. A defendant is always innocent until there is absolutely no doubt of guilt. And there is no doubt in my mind that the defendant is innocent. Thank you."

"Pretty short," Emily whispers, sounding worried.

"Nice and short," I reply. Maybe too short.

Goode is smiling and makes a V sign with his fingers to his secretary.

That's not a good omen.

CHAPTER 12

"You may call your first witness," Judge Wolf says, glancing at Goode. "I call Sir Lance A. Little," Goode announces in his rich baritone. Two bear-heads begin pushing 'the mummy' in a wheelchair up to the witness box.

"Sir Lancalittle?" I ask my uncle. "Is he the knight in the King Arthur stories?"

"You read about King Arthur?" Uncle Jasper looks surprised.

"I saw the movie."

"Not as good," he mutters. "And not the same knight. Not at all."

I get what my uncle means. This knight is a mess. Only his face isn't covered in bandages. His eyes are droopy, his mustache looks like a scrawny, black caterpillar with down-turned ends reaching below his hairless chin, and his cheeks are gray hollows. "This guy is a knight?"

"He's the victim."

"Oh, boy. We're in a heap of trouble."

"Agreed."

The knight is wheeled to the front of the courtroom as I hear gasps from the gallery. When he gets to the front, it takes two knights to lift him and gently place him on the witness chair. They hold him upright as a third knight snaps a safety harness around his middle to keep him steady. He lets out a blast of coughing.

"Your sight fills me with fear. Are you well enough to be here?" Judge Wolf asks.

The witness replies in a wheezy voice. "My duty calls." He bursts into another fit of coughing.

"I'll be short, your honor," Hugh B. Goode says.

"He's a giant, how can he be short?" I joke to Emily.

She digs her fingernails into my arm.

"Hey, you did that last time. Stop it!" I yank my arm off the table.

"I get nervous," she whispers.

But does she apologize? Guess.

Goode approaches the witness. "You are Sir. Lance A. Little, the victim?"

The knight coughs twice. "Y...yes."

My uncle shouts, "Objection."

The judge says. "Objection sustained. Mr. Good, please use 'alleged' because, at this time, the defendant is innocent until you prove he did it."

I look at Emily. "That means the judge agrees with my uncle."

Emily smirks. "Brodie, I know that already."

She knows everything. I'm sorry I tried to help her.

"Can you describe what happened on the date in question?" Goode asks.

The knight closes his eyes and speaks very low, in broken sentences. "I was riding... on my... horse...poor Hamlet...I knew him well..." He bursts into tears.

"Can you proceed? More time do you need?" The judge asks.

The knight sniffles. "We were on the Zig-Zag Skyway...suddenly, out of nowhere, I see...I see...I see..." The knight's eyes open wide, and his right hand raises ever so slowly. He points to the cage with a bandaged finger. "I see...that monster!"

"Objection, your honor!" Uncle Jasper shouts. "My client is not a monster. Every defendant's right not to be called names must be enforced."

The judge sighs. "Mr. Little, please do not call this defendant any names. We must respect all defendants' rights, even dragons."

The knight nods. "When we train... to defend Monstrovia... they call these creatures... monsters. I'll try... to remember... but it's hard after...a whole life... of training... and thousands... of books that call them... monsters."

He's prejudiced against dragons. So was I. He's right about one thing: it is hard to change when all your life you're taught to hate something. While

I'm still afraid of some of Monstrovia's 'unique' residents, I think I'm getting better. I've learned some horrible looking creatures have kind and noble hearts, like the Serpentake, and Horace, while some beautiful creatures are the most terrible monsters of all. *Darn! I missed some questions. I've got to focus.* That's another thing I've learned: the tiniest detail can sometimes win a case. A good lawyer pays attention to every word, emotion, and physical reaction of the witness.

Goode helps the knight blow his nose and then asks, "So the dragon allegedly just "plowed" into you, without any provocation, and knocked you off your horse?"

"He just charged right… into me. He done it… on purpose…knocked me on my butt. I saw hate in his eyes. I knew I was a goner, your honor."

There's a buzz in the gallery, spectators glaring at Horace. They believe the knight.

Goode waits for silence. "What happened to Hamlet, your horse?"

"My horse…my poor little horsie…" The knight trembles. "Thrown clear off the skyway. He's gone… gone… gone."

"He's another goner, your honor," Goode says, wiping a tear from his eye with a red, white, and blue handkerchief that matches his American flag tie.

"He's gone to the great beyond," the judge says, shaking his head sadly. "A knight without a horse is useless in battle, of course."

Uncle Jasper looks ready to object but decides to sit quietly.

Goode walks back to his table and picks up a large poster mounted on cardboard. He holds it in front of the gallery and then brings it to the witness. "Do you recognize the subject of this photograph?"

The knight's voice cracks. "That's me…before the…assassination—"

"Alleged, please?" Judge Wolf interrupts.

"Alleged? Alleged… assassination by that… dragon." Sir Little's voice is teary. "I was beautiful… so beautiful…"

I expect tears with all the knight's sobbing but see nothing. Maybe I'm too far from him. I write on my pad and shove it in front of Uncle Jasper. "No tears?"

Uncle Jasper doesn't react. He also doesn't object. Normally, a lawyer may object when the opposing lawyer says something that isn't important to the case. He can also object if a witness gives an opinion rather than a fact. I would have objected, but Uncle Jasper says sometimes it's better not to call attention to what a witness says. You hope the judge, or jury, doesn't remember it or know themselves it isn't real evidence. Being a lawyer takes a lot of careful listening. Emily could never do it because she talks too much. I glance at her and see she's taking notes on a yellow pad just like mine. Hmmm? I could be wrong about her.

Goode walks around the courtroom with the large photo of Sir Lance A Little, the way he looked before the accident.

There are surprised gasps as people compare the portrait of the glorious knight in shining armor, mounted proudly on his battle steed, to this wreck of a mummified man.

One woman says, "Oh, that poor man. I would have loved to ride off to his castle with him…but not now."

Another woman, snorts and growls, "That dragon should be boiled in oil for what he did to Prince Charming here."

"I feel sorry for Sir Little," Emily whispers.

"We're doomed," I whisper to my uncle.

He nods his head and says, "I know."

CHAPTER 13

U ncle Jasper has a habit of drawing when things aren't going well. He already has a bunch of doodles on his legal pad.

Mr. Goode is back in front of the witness. "After the accident, did the dragon stop to help you…to check you out?"

"No. He was gone." The knight coughs hard. "He didn't… care about the damage… he didn't care. He just… flew off."

"So, you were left on your own until help arrived?" Goode looks terribly sorry for the knight.

"Alone, you survived until help arrived?" Judge Wolf asks and shakes his head sadly.

"Yes. I was… in terrible pain. Look at me… these bandages. How could you leave me like that?"

A knight raises his armored fist and shouts, "Down with dragons! Down with dragons!"

The other knights stomp their boots, raise their fists, and echo the chant, "Down with dragons! Down with—"

Judge Wolf is roaring mad. He slams the gavel down hard on his desk. "Enough! No more of this stuff! Be silent in my courtroom row, or all of you out will go!"

The knights return to their seats, meek as lambs under the judge's wolfish gaze.

"Objection!" Uncle Jasper says when things are calm again. He doesn't bother standing.

The judge glares at the knights again and says, "Objection sustained. Mr.

Little, please do not address the defendant. That's something you mustn't do. You should only answer the questions as they're asked of you."

"I can't be... honest?"

"Yes, of course, we want you to tell what is true, but don't speak to the defendant, since he's not allowed to answer you."

"I'll try... but that uncaring beast did leave me... to die. That's no...lie."

"I promise you he will be punished for his crimes. But at the right times." The judge glares at Horace.

I can't understand why Uncle Jasper isn't hopping mad at the judge for obviously deciding Horace is guilty, but he is staring hard at his doodles.

Goode seems surprised too, looking as if he's waiting for Uncle Jasper to say something, then he continues. "Sir Little, have you ever seen this defendant before?"

"Yes...yes, I have."

"Can you tell us when you saw him before this incident?"

"About two years ago. I was bringing... another evil dragon to court—"

Uncle Jasper raises his hand. "Objection, your honor. We're not interested in knowing about another dragon."

The judge snarls, "Overruled. I'm very interested in knowing if the knight knew the defendant prior to this accident."

Uncle Jasper hisses, "We're in trouble."

Goode smiles. "Let's forget about the other dragon. Just tell us what you witnessed."

Uncle Jasper looks like he's trying to think of anything to object to, but is coming up dry.

Emily writes something on her pad and slides it to my uncle.

"Objection, your honor. If the prosecution is going to mention another possible crime, that may prejudice the court." He glances at Emily and whispers, "Thank you."

Emily smiles at me, not as if she swallowed a canary, but a whole dozen of those twittering pests.

She's such a 'know-it-all,' but at least, she's on our side.

The judge bares his teeth, showing he's all-wolf when he has to be. "Are you saying, in your sneaky way, that I can be by prejudice swayed?" He leans over the bench, a powerful and scary figure. "I am sworn to be fair, so have a care. Nothing influences my thought. I can't be swayed and can't be bought." He is so far across the bench I'm afraid he's going to fall over. Would that be so bad? We'd get a different judge.

Uncle Jasper backs away. "No, of course not, your honor, but if a defendant has a criminal record, it can't be brought up in court. It is a violation of his rights."

Goode nods. "I know that, your honor. But you see nobody brought Horace to the police, or court, for this act. So, he has no record. And it happened so long ago that we can't put him on trial for it anyway."

Uncle Jasper's hands grip the table. "Your honor, I strongly object to this line of questioning, which is meant to prejudice you against the defendant."

What can be so bad?

The judge stares with rage at Horace in the cage. "I believe Mr. Goode has made a good point. Since the defendant cannot be tried for the alleged crime, because of the passage of time. Though I have indigestion, I'm going to allow the question. But, Mr. Goode, I will want to see the importance of this question, or I will sustain Doofinch's objection."

Uncle Jasper shakes his head. "This is bad, really bad."

"His poetry?" I ask, thinking it's really awful.

Emily leans toward me. "The Judge is allowing the question because Horace wasn't arrested."

"I know," I hiss. "Shhh."

Goode walks back to his table, and his secretary hands him another photograph on a large cardboard sheet. "Do you recognize this?" He displays the photo to the court and the witness.

My stomach churns. I know what's coming.

The knight replies in a surprisingly loud voice. "That is the statue of the greatest knight of all... the first Dragonslayer, our hero, our role model!"

Emily digs her fingernails into my arm.

I pry her loose.

Goode smiles broadly. "Can you tell us what you saw when you approached

45

the courthouse on September 15, two years ago?"

"Objection! How can he remember what happened on the exact date so long ago?"

"Because I was shocked, horrified… disgusted. That dragon… the one in the cage…was cursing, stomping…screaming… and then…and then… he tried to pull down… the statue of the Dragonslayer. Shame on you! Shame on you!"

All the knights in the gallery are on their feet and screaming at Horace, "Shame on you! Shame on you!"

I glance out the window. The great Dragonslayer statue is standing in the middle of the courtyard. A vision flashes before my eyes. Horace is reaching up and pulling the mighty statue to the ground. There is an explosive crash. Pieces are lying on the dirt. The Dragonslayer's severed head is in Horace's clawed hands.

CHAPTER 14

Even the judge looks shocked, rising from his chair. "You tried to pull down the statue of the great Dragonslayer?"

"I warned Horace not to do that," Uncle Jasper hisses at me.

"Sweet, kind, Horace really did that?" Emily asks me.

"I guess," I reply.

The knights are enraged, stomping their boots and chanting, "Down with dragons! Long live the Dragonslayer!"

"Order in the court!" The judge shouts, bangs his gavel, and shouts again, "Order in the court! Order in the court!"

The room becomes silent again.

Judge Wolf stands on his desk and roars, "While I share your dismay. No more shouting or stomping today. Behave yourselves, I warn you. This vicious dragon will get his due."

"Did you hear that?" I ask my uncle. "He hates dragons too."

"Shhh," Uncle Jasper says, giving me a warning look.

Goode beams and continues, "Sir Little, you witnessed this disgrace yourself?"

"Alleged disgrace," Uncle Jasper mutters.

Goode shakes his head and repeats, "Alleged disgrace. You saw it?"

"I did. I was shocked, horrified, disgusted. This dragon was so full of... hate."

Uncle Jasper bounces to his feet. "Objection! Unless Sir Little can read minds, he can't possibly know if anyone is "full of hate.""

The knight wags his finger at Horace. "He kept screaming, "I hate knights!

I hate knights! Doesn't that mean... he hates ...knights?"

Uncle Jasper warned me many times to never ask a question if you don't know the answer you're going to get. I think this is a great example of why a lawyer should always try to be sure he knows what a witness is going to say before he asks questions.

"Objection! How do we know Horace really said that? It's only your word against Horace's. How do we know who to believe?" Uncle Jasper is almost shouting at the witness.

"The prisoner he was escorting to court heard it too," Goode says, a smug gloat on his face. "The prisoner was, by the way, another dragon. Do you want me to call this other dragon as a witness?"

Uncle Jasper looks trapped. "Let's finish with this witness first," he mutters, making a doodle of a thumbs-down on his pad.

Goode casts another smile at my uncle. It's like a harpoon shot at my uncle. "If you saw the defendant trying to take down the statue, why didn't you stop him?"

"I was going to ask that, "Uncle Jasper whispers.

A good lawyer anticipates what his opponent may ask. Goode is doing a good job of cutting my uncle off before he can ask anything that will hurt his witness.

The knight sighs. "I would have stopped him. You must remember I was guarding...another prisoner. I couldn't do... nothin' with another vicious...dragon...to guard."

Goode flips over his pad. "Thank you, Sir Little, for your testimony and your brave service." He whirls gracefully to face my uncle. "Your turn, Doofinch...ha-ha...the Defender."

I could punch out his lights, but then I'd be in trouble.

Uncle Jasper looks uncertainly at me, shrugs, and then walks toward the witness stand. "Did Horace actually succeed in pulling down the statue?"

"No. Nothing can pull down the Dragonslayer," He raises his fist to his buddies in the gallery and they raise theirs.

Judge Wolf shoots them a stern look and raises h is gavel. All the fists drop.

Uncle Jasper turns back to the bandaged knight. "So, the Dragonslayer statue was not pulled down or broken. Sir Little, after you allegedly witnessed Horace trying to topple the statue, what did you do?"

"What do… you mean?"

"You said you were guarding another dragon, but once you delivered the dragon to court, what did you do?"

I glance at Goode. He seems uninterested, leaning back in his chair. Uncle's right, the slimeball is too confident.

Sir Little says, "I sat in the… courtroom until I was needed… again."

"You did your job? Your duty?"

"I always… do," the knight replies, "At least… until this happened… to me." He holds up a bandaged arm. "He did…this…to me."

"But isn't it also your duty to stop crime?"

"I already explained—"

Uncle Jasper interrupts. "You said you had to take the dragon to the courtroom. But once you did that, shouldn't you have reported the crime you allegedly witnessed?"

"He's nailing him," Emily says. "Go, Doofinch, go!"

"Shhh," I reply, not wanting to miss any of this.

"Your honor, the defense is attacking the witness," Goode says, still looking comfortable.

Uncle Jasper is also very calm. "Not at all, your honor. I'm just trying to understand why a knight, sworn to prevent crimes, never reported this serious incident that he allegedly witnessed. You never did report it. Did you?"

The knight coughs and shifts slightly in his seat. "No."

"So, there aren't any written records anywhere that this alleged crime took place?"

The knight's voice is shrill. "You're calling me a liar? Do you think I made this up?" He strains to rise from the chair, his fist shaking in anger. "I didn't make it up! I saw him! I saw him!"

"He saw him! He saw him!" The knights shout until Judge Wolf raises his gavel.

Goode is out of his chair. "Your honor. I'd like a short recess."

Uncle Jasper smiles. "I'd like to continue. If I may?"

The judge looks at the wall clock. "We'll recess for ten minutes."

"You got him," I whisper to my uncle.

"You did great," Emily says.

Uncle Jasper sits on his chair. "He did it," he says softly. "Horace did try to pull down that blasted statue." He looks at me. "You see, Brodie, Emily, this is one of the hard parts about being a lawyer. Even if you know your client did something, you must try and convince the jury, in this case, the judge, that he might not have."

"But that's your job. You've got to try your best for the defendant. Everyone understands that. I do now too." At first, I thought it was wrong to defend someone you think may be guilty, but now I understand that the first rule of being a lawyer is doing your best to make sure your client gets a fair trial.

Uncle Jasper brushes down his fly-away hair. "You're right, I have to do whatever I can to help my client. But when you know that they did something wrong, that makes it tough." He turns toward the knight, being wheeled from the courtroom. "I hate trying to convince Wolf, and everyone else, that this unfortunate knight is a liar. I can't allow the judge to accept his story."

Emily looks puzzled. "Why is it so important that Horace tried to pull down that statue?"

Wow! I finally know something she doesn't. I hope I'm not smiling too much. I don't want her to think I'm gloating. I clear my throat. "Emily, if the knight's story is true, it means Horace hates knights. If he hates them so much, then he might have wanted to kill Sir Little. It gives him a motive for driving right into Sir Little's horse."

Uncle Jasper nods. "Brodie's right. Pulling down that stupid statue would be proof that Horace hates knights enough to want to kill them. Now, they have no proof he pulled down that statue." He sighs. "I just feel sad that I made that knight look bad, after all, he was telling the truth. I made it seem as if he wasn't." He looks at Emily. "I know it makes me look like a bad guy, but I have to do what I can. I just hate adding to Sir Little's suffering."

"Would you like me to check on Sir Little?" Emily asks.

"That might make me feel better," Uncle Jasper replies.

"I'll be back," Emily says and then turns toward me. "Do you want to come with me, Brodie?"

Am I blushing? "No, thank you. I'll stay here with my Uncle."

Uncle Jasper shakes his head. "You should go with her."

I really hope I'm not blushing. "So, do you think we won?" I ask, wondering why he still looks worried.

"Not yet. But things are looking a little better."

"Then why is Goode still smiling like a giant alligator?" I see the lawyer chatting with some pixie photographers and handing out autographs to people in the gallery.

"I wish I knew," Uncle Jasper replies.

My focus is on a group of knights. They are in a corner of the room, but every so often, I see one of them aiming his eyes at my uncle. And they are not friendly looks.

CHAPTER 15

The knight in bandages is back on the stand, and Uncle Jasper is raring to go. "Let's get to the day of the accident." He signals me with his hand, and I set up a large diagram of the accident scene. "You were in the right lane, heading east. Is that correct?"

"Yes. I was going…home."

"You were heading home. From where?"

"I was… with friends."

"I didn't ask, with who? I asked, where were you heading home from?"

"Oh. I misunderstood. I was coming from the Dead Dragon… Inn." The knight stops talking and then says quickly, "I mean, I was at an inn."

Uncle Jasper's voice is like syrup. "Now, now. You are under oath. Please tell us exactly where you were just before the accident?"

"Well, it wasn't just before—"

"I repeat, where were you coming from?" Uncle Jasper is now standing directly in front of the knight. "Let me repeat what you said. You said you were coming from the—"

"Inn. The inn. Okay?" The knight sounds angry.

Uncle Jasper smiles. "What inn was that, again?"

"Objection!" Goode is standing for this one.

"Overruled," the judge says. "Spectators, hold your din, I want the name of the inn."

"What was the name of the inn?" Uncle Jasper is now inches from the knight's bandaged face.

The knight coughs loudly, his entire body convulsing violently.

"Are you okay today?" Judge Wolf leans over the witness stand.

The knight doesn't answer. He's still shaking and coughing.

Uncle Jasper waits patiently and then says, "The name of the inn, Sir Little?"

The knight looks like he's waiting for help from Goode, but it isn't coming. He wipes his nose and says in a low voice, "The D…D…Dead… Dragon."

"The what?" Uncle Jasper asks, but I know he heard. Everyone in the room heard.

"The Dead Dragon." The knight repeats, and quickly adds, "It's just where all the knights… gather."

"At the Dead Dragon Inn?" Uncle Jasper looks at the judge. "Interesting name. I wonder who hates who?"

"Objection!" Goode looks furious.

"Sustained. Mr. Doofinch, keep your comments to yourself, please?" The judge says.

"Sorry, your honor. What were you doing at the Dead Dragon Inn?" Uncle Jasper leans on the railing of the witness box.

Goode is up again. "Objection! What does that have to do with this case?"

"Overruled. I'd like to know what Sir Little was doing just before the accident."

"Your uncle is amazing. He's doing great," Emily whispers.

I smile.

Uncle Jasper repeats the question. "What were you doing at the Dead Dragon Inn?"

"I don't remember. The accident gave me… partial amnesia."

Uncle Jasper makes a face. "Partial amnesia? Hmmm? We'll have to call your doctor about that. But you remember you were at the Dead Dragon Inn?"

"Yes."

"I can call some of your friends to the stand and ask them what you usually do at the Dead Dragon Inn." Uncle Jasper says.

Goode is up again. "Objection! He's threatening the witness."

"Overruled. Telling Sir Little, he plans to call other witnesses is not a threat. You did it before."

Goode sits down.

Uncle Jasper continues. "Sir Little, what do you knights usually do at the Dead Dragon Inn?"

Sir Little hesitates. I think he's waiting for another objection. When it doesn't come, he replies, "We talk. That's all."

"So, when you're at the Dead Dragon Inn, you talk. About what?"

"Objection!"

"Overruled. Please stop slowing down this trial? Without a jury, you can safely assume I know the law and will act on my own to stop anything I feel isn't correct legal procedure."

Goode slumps slightly. "Sorry, your honor. I'm just doing my job."

"Good, Goode. But you should realize I'm aware of what is proper questioning and will do my job."

Goode nods again.

Uncle Jasper continues, "Okay, Sir Little, what do you knights talk about so long? By the way, how long do most of these sessions last?" Uncle Jasper looks genuinely interested.

"I don't know...a few minutes..."

"You go all the way into the forest, to the Dead Dragon Inn, and stay only a few minutes?"

I love the way my uncle listens to every answer and then twists it into a question to trip up the witness. So cool.

"It's not that far."

"How far is it?"

"I don't know. Maybe ...five or six miles...."

"So, you travel five miles by horseback, to get to the Dead Dragon Inn, to talk for a few minutes?" Uncle Jasper shrugs his shoulders as if he finds this hard to believe.

"Well, maybe it's more than a few minutes?"

"Is it a half-hour? How about one hour? Two hours? Three or four?"

"Yeah. Okay. I'd say about an hour...sometimes two."

I swear I feel the sweat dripping off Sir Little as my uncle is grilling him with all these questions. Great job, Uncle, I'm thinking. It's over. Horace is safe.

CHAPTER 16

E mily slides her pad to me. On it, she wrote, "I wish your uncle would stop saying the name of that Inn so much. It's annoying."

I write back, "He wants the judge to remember that awful name, "Dead Dragon." Smart strategy."

Uncle Jasper picks up a file folder from our table and holds it closed in his hand. "What if I told you there are witnesses who will say that most times you stay at the Dead Dragon for two to three hours, and more? Is that accurate?"

"I guess. I don't have a watch in my armor." Little laughs.

A few knights laugh, but most of the gallery is silent. Some of the knights are restless. A few are glaring daggers at my uncle.

"No watch in your armor? That's funny." Uncle Jasper chuckles, but then fires another question, "So, you agree it could be a couple of hours?"

"Sure. Fine. What difference does it make?"

"The Dead Dragon Inn looks like a nice place." Uncle Jasper holds up a large photo of the front of the inn. "I like the sign. Is that a dead dragon?"

"I wouldn't know. I ain't the artist."

Uncle Jasper shows the poster again around the courtroom. He then holds it up for the judge to see and quietly asks, "Does the Dead Dragon Inn have a bar?"

"What inn doesn't have a bar?" The knight laughs again.

"What inn doesn't have a bar?" A few knights repeat and laugh. One calls my uncle, a "moron."

"Objection, your honor!" Goode is on his feet. "I know where Doofinch is going with this!"

"Good, then you'll let him get there without any more interruptions," Judge Wolf says, glaring at Goode.

Goode drops to his chair.

"So, the Dead Dragon Inn has a bar. And you're at the Dead Dragon Inn several hours. Is that right?"

"I said so already."

"And most of the time, you're talking to other knights?"

"They're my brothers."

I notice Sir Little is more capable of full sentences than before.

"Do you talk about old times?"

The judge interrupts. "Mr. Doofinch, is it really important what they talk about in this inn?"

"I believe it is, your honor." Uncle Jasper waits, and the judge nods. "Do you talk about old times?"

"Yes."

"What we call 'war stories?'"

"I suppose."

"Do you talk about your accomplishments? I mean, you're all brave knights."

"Thank you for saying that. Yes, we're proud of our accomplishments."

"And you should be. Knights do many wonderful deeds to help Monstrovia." He smiles at the gallery and then turns back to Little. "Do you share stories about your battles?"

"Yes, of course. That is a big part of our history."

"Battles with enemy armies?"

"Yes."

"Battles with other men?"

"Yes. Those who fought enemy knights deserve to have their stories told."

"Battles with dragons?"

"Yes. Dragons are among our most vicious opponents."

"Down with dragons!" A knight shouts from the last row.

"Remove that man now!" Judge Wolf shouts, and two bear-heads rush to the last row. They stand by the knight, and he raises his gloved fist in the air as he's escorted from the court.

"Be sure he leaves the building," the judge says.

I feel a tingle of victory. Uncle Jasper has given Sir Little one question after another to lead him into the trap. I think the knight knows it. It's like walking into quicksand: he's going to sink, and there's nothing he can do to stop it. Even Goode is powerless.

Uncle Jasper glances at Horace and smiles. "Isn't it true that members of your order are sworn to kill dragons?"

"Dragons are evil. These ugly firebreathers have been a danger to mankind...since time began."

"I understand how you feel. You've been taught to hate dragons."

"They're deadly. Dragons kill defenseless men, women, and children!"

"All dragons?"

"Look in your books! They're monsters! They destroy anyone who gets in their way. We risk our lives to protect you, people. We're the good guys!"

"And all dragons are the bad guys?"

The knight screams, "You know the truth! You're just twisting everything around! That dragon tried to kill me and then left me to die! Yes, I hunt dragons. But only to protect all those who could become their victims." He gets quiet, his eyes rolling up to the ceiling.

"Are you a Dragonslayer?" Uncle Jasper asks.

Emily shoots me a question mark on her pad.

"A secret society of knights," I write back.

Little is staring at the ceiling.

"Are you alright?" Uncle Jasper asks, an alarmed look on his face. "Your honor!"

Two guards rush up as the knight bursts into a fit of coughing, body shaking violently.

"He needs help," a guard shouts. "Call 9-1-1!"

Sir Little's eyes roll up and his head rocks hard from side to side.

"He's having a seizure," someone screams.

"He's dying," someone else yells.

"Clear the courtroom!" Judge Wolf orders. "Now! Everyone, out!" He glares at my uncle. "Lawyers too! Out! Out!"

"You did it!" I whisper to my uncle as we hurry from the room. "You showed the judge that Sir Little was full of hate for dragons."

Uncle Jasper stops me in the hallway. "Brodie, what I did was destroy a good man."

Emily frowns. "You really believe he's a good man?"

"I do. Sir Little's belief that all dragons are bad doesn't necessarily make him a bad person. He's been taught that since his birth. He believes he is helping people, and he's willing to risk his life for that. And I may have killed him."

"But he's wrong. He's prejudiced," I say, confused by my uncle's reaction.

"He is wrong, but I'm a knight too." Uncle Jasper points to a pin, a tiny sword, on his lapel.

"You're a knight? For real?"

"You've seen the portrait of me wearing armor in my office. Why are you so surprised?"

I never thought he was a real knight. I guess I should have. "Are you a Dragonslayer too?"

"Of course not. Not all knights are Dragonslayers. Not all knights belong to that club." He sighs. "But that man is my brother. I feel as if I'm destroying a brother, a fellow knight, who is willing to sacrifice his life for what he believes. And now, I have to do even more damage to him and my order if I want to save Horace…if I didn't kill him already?"

As we wait outside the room, a group of knights is nearby. Some glare at us. One walks over and says, "Doofinch, I heard you just now. You say you're a knight? You should be ashamed of yourself." He holds his fist in Uncle Jasper's face. "You just be careful, traitor."

A few of the other knights hold up their gloved fists.

A pair of bear-head guards step between us and the knights.

"I don't think your brother likes you much," I whisper as the knight walks back to his friends, and I hear them laughing.

"I think you're right," Uncle Jasper says. "I don't like myself much right now."

A siren screeches loudly, and four bear-heads in white suits come racing past.

"Where's the patient," a bear-head asks, staring at me as if I'm an alien, which in this place, I am.

"The knight is in the courtroom. Hurry," Uncle Jasper says.

"You that lawyer?" One of the medics asks, baring his teeth.

My uncle nods. "Do you need help, my friend?"

The bear-head snarls, "I wish it was you in there who needs my help."

Uncle Jasper backs away. "You'd better hurry. The poor man needs you badly."

"Lucky for you, lawyer."

Uncle Jasper smiles at me. "I guess not everyone likes me. Eh?"

I wonder how the Judge will feel if Sir Little is taken to the hospital after my uncle fired questions at him. I can hear him saying, "It's all your fault, Doofinch. All your fault."

"What happens if Sir Little can't continue," I ask my uncle who looks as if he's the one who had the seizure.

"I don't know. I just hope he can. I'd hate to have it on my conscience that I caused a fellow knight to die."

CHAPTER 17

After about ten dragon-swallows, the judge calls us back into the courtroom.

Uncle Jasper is nervous. "I hope Sir Little is okay," he mutters.

The judge glares down from his desk. "Hrumph. No help from you, Doofinch, but Sir Little is better now. The Monstrovian medics say it was a panic attack." He looks at my uncle, his wolf eyebrows knit close together. "Sir Little has been severely weakened by his condition. Doofinch, you will be more considerate as you proceed. If you must proceed?"

Uncle Jasper breathes a huge sigh of relief. "Thank you, your honor."

The judge signals the bear-head clerk. "Escort Sir Little back into the room. Let's hope Doofinch doesn't drive him to his doom."

My uncle looks badly shaken as he watches Sir Little being wheeled back to the witness stand. Once the knight is strapped in, Uncle Jasper gives him a friendly smile. "Sir Little, I'm glad you're feeling better. Are you well enough to answer a few more questions?"

The mummified knight coughs twice.

Goode, still seated, says, "Two coughs mean yes."

Jasper sighs. "Two coughs. Okay. We've established that you usually spend an hour or more at the Dead Dragon Inn."

"Cough. Cough."

"Talking with your friends."

"Cough. Cough."

"And you were there just before your accident?"

"Cough. Cough."

"Talking for a couple of hours can make you thirsty. Can't it?"

"Doofinch, really?" Goode is out of his seat objecting. "Your honor—"

"Mr. Doofinch, everyone would agree that talking for a couple of hours would make one thirsty, so let's get to your point, please? I'm getting thirsty myself."

"Yes, your honor. Don't you get thirsty when you're talking for a long while?"

"What?" The knight explodes. "I don't drink."

"I see you're feeling better," Uncle Jasper says.

The knight stammers. "Y...yes."

"So, you can talk now?"

"Y...yes. I guess so."

"Good. So, back to the Dead Dragon Inn. Everyone gets thirsty after talking a long while. I'm thirsty now—"

"I don't drink too much. I know what you're driving at," the knight says.

"Not much, you say? Well, how much do you drink then?" Uncle Jasper asks.

"What?" The knight looks confused.

"You said you don't drink "too much," but that means you do drink."

"He's nailing him with his own words," Emily says.

"Lawyers listen," I reply, wishing she'd stop talking and listen for a change.

The knight looks anxious. "I...I...I don't get drunk! I don't drink that much!"

"Enough! That's it!" Goode springs from his seat, arms waving. "Your honor, this is going too far! He's attacking this poor man! He's calling him a drunk!"

Uncle Jasper replies in an unruffled tone, "I'm not calling him anything. He said, "I don't drink too much." That means he drinks. All I'm doing is following up on his admission that he does drink."

"Your honor, I protest this whole thing. May I see you in chambers?"

"Any objection, Mr. Doofinch?"

"No, your honor."

The judge walks behind his desk and scoots out a door in the wall.

Goode shakes his fist at my uncle and storms out a side door.

I lean toward my uncle. "You are accusing him of drinking, aren't you?"

He replies, "I don't like doing that, but I have a strategy. My goal is to try and prove that Horace is not entirely responsible for the accident. In other words, that the other driver was also at fault." He hurries to follow Goode into the judge's chambers.

"Can he do that?" Emily asks.

"I think so. Uncle Jasper knocked out the accusation that Horace tried to destroy that statue, so they have no real proof that he hates knights. That means they have no motive for him to deliberately kill Sir Little."

"So, it was an accident?" Emily looks unconvinced.

"Well, if they can't prove Horace had a reason to plow into Sir Little, that really helps.

Goode is frowning when he stomps back into the courtroom a few minutes later. He throws himself into his seat and searches through the pile of papers in front of him.

"The judge is considering Goode's objection," Uncle Jasper says when he returns a few seconds later. "I don't know how it's going to go, but keep your fingers crossed."

"Emily doesn't understand your strategy," I say, getting one-up on her for a change.

Emily gives me a dirty look and says, "Brodie says that now that you knocked out the idea that Horace hates knights, you're trying to prove it was just an accident. Can you do that?"

Uncle Jasper smiles at her. "Brody is right. I think the judge will agree to that. The problem is that they're still saying it was all Horace's fault. Horace could still end up in prison."

Emily listens silently. "I didn't know any of this."

My uncle smiles. "Most young people don't know much about the law, but at least you're willing to learn. Okay, so I want to prove that Horace isn't completely at fault. That's called "contributory negligence." Are you familiar with that?"

Uncle Jasper likes to fool me with hard legal terms. Some I know, but a lot of others I never heard of. I like learning them, though. "I know what negligence means. It's like if I don't do something I was supposed to do."

"That's good. Can you give me an example?"

"Like if I don't throw away a banana peel and someone slips on it. Leaving the peel, there, wasn't trying to be bad, just negligent, careless."

Uncle Jasper laughs. "Good example. You didn't mean to cause an accident, but by not doing something, you did cause one. It is serious if someone gets hurt slipping on that banana peel." He scratches his chin. "Now, let's take your example and add one twist. What does it mean when you 'contribute' to an accident?"

Emily jumps in. I should have known her not knowing something wouldn't last. "Contribute means you give something...like you "contribute" to a charity."

"Right." Uncle Jasper smiles at her again. "When you contribute to an accident, it means something you did helped cause the accident, even if you weren't the main cause."

"So, it's like 'double negligence,' where both are to blame?" I jump in before Emily can reply.

Uncle Jasper spreads out his folders and his notepad. "I guess you could say that. In your banana example, let's say the man who slipped on the banana peel was reading a book while walking."

"That would be pretty stupid," I say.

"That would be contributory negligence. The victim helped cause the accident even if he wasn't completely at fault."

"Wait a minute? That means when Principal Feeney parked his car in a place where there was a lot of mud around—"

Uncle Jasper groans. "No. Absolutely not. Throwing mudballs at your principal's car is a 'deliberate' act, so it's a crime. Doing something on purpose, my aspiring lawyer, is not negligence. It is a crime. So, forget the mudballs forever."

"You threw mudballs at your principal's car?" Emily looks shocked and then bursts into laughter. "I knew you were crazy, but—"

Uncle Jasper glares at her. "Miss Beanstalk, please do not make light of my

64

nephew's poor judgment before he came under my positive influence. For your information, both of you, if his principal had wanted to, and he must be a good man to not do so, he could have filed a complaint with the police. My young rascal of a nephew would have needed a good lawyer of his own."

"I'm sorry," Emily mutters, looking embarrassed.

"And he could never be accepted as a lawyer with a criminal record. So, I sincerely hope that both of you will steer clear of any more such 'brilliant' ideas." He stares at Emily with his most penetrating Perry Mason eyes, "Is that clear?"

Emily gulps, the first time I've ever seen her humbled by anyone. "Yes, sir," she replies and shoots me an angry look.

Like it was my fault?

"Good. Now, when the judge returns, I want you both to pay close attention. There's something about this whole case that doesn't add up."

Emily's staring straight ahead. I don't think she's used to getting a scolding, nor a lecture. I almost feel sorry for her. Almost.

When the judge returns, he isn't smiling.

CHAPTER 18

Judge Wolf looks really mad, and he's rhyming again. "Your questions, Doofinch, have put Goode in a funk. I believe you're implying Sir Little is a drunk."

"That's bad. Wolf is rhyming again," I whisper to Emily.

She doesn't reply. She's staring straight ahead.

I don't know if she's frightened or just angry with me. It isn't my fault she got in trouble.

Uncle Jasper stands and calmly replies, "Your honor, I'm not trying to prove Sir Little is a drunk, just asking questions about the afternoon of the accident."

Judge Wolf shows his teeth. "I believe you're entitled to do what you must, but I warn you, don't abuse my trust."

Uncle Jasper whispers to me, "This is bad. The judge is mad."

Goode looks smug. I guess he's satisfied.

Uncle Jasper hefts up his trousers and walks toward the knight. "Sir Little, I only have a few more questions. I want it made clear that my questions are not about you as a man, nor your reputation as a knight. I only want to know about the afternoon of the accident." He checks the judge's face.

There's still an angry scowl on the judge's wooly face.

Uncle Jasper pats down his wispy hair. "Sir, we know you were in the Dead Dragon Inn with your fellow knights for about two to three hours on the day of the accident. We also know you were talking, and there is a bar in the inn. It is natural to get thirsty under such circumstances, so please tell us what you drank that afternoon?" He waits, and when there is no answer, he adds, "We can ask the bartender who was working that day."

The knight coughs. "I had a beer."

"One? More?"

"I don't know. It could have been two."

"Could it have been three?"

The knight hesitates, head twitching. "I don't know. Maybe."

"If you were there for three hours, could it have been four?"

Goode is on his feet and roaring at the judge. "Your honor, he's doing it again."

The judge sighs. "Doofinch, what did I say? You can't continue in this way."

Uncle Jasper looks at me and then says, "It's natural for someone who has been talking in a bar for several hours to have a few drinks. In this case, how many is important."

The judge closes his eyes and then opens them. "Here's what I'm now thinking. I'll allow your questions about his drinking. Drinking is bad before you drive a car, of course, but just don't push this point too far about drinking and driving a horse."

Goode sags in his seat but quickly sits up again.

Uncle Jasper checks his notes. "If you were at the Dead Dragon Inn for three hours, could you have had four beers?"

The knight looks at Goode, but the lawyer shows no reaction. Little coughs and finally replies, "No. Never four. I always stop at three." He shakes his head. "I never drink more than three when I'm going to drive home on my horse. I guess I had three. No more, for sure."

There's a murmur in the courtroom. It's as if everyone knows the case is over, and Uncle Jasper has won, but he isn't letting up. "You said you always stop at three beers. Why is that?"

"I don't know. I kind of feel like if I have more, I'll feel unsteady."

"But at three, you feel okay to drive?"

"Sure. I do it all the time."

"And you've never had an accident before?"

"What do you mean?"

"Objection! Whether or not Sir Little has had a previous accident has nothing to do with this case."

Judge Wolf looks at his paws. One has claws fully extended, not a good sign. "Overruled. As in your earlier explanation about Horace allegedly pulling down the Dragonslayer statue, since no previous crime is involved, I see no reason why this question shouldn't be allowed."

Uncle Jasper whispers to me, "He's stopped rhyming. That's better. I hope." He turns back to the knight. "Have you had other accidents before this one?"

"No. I have a spotless record."

"No drunk driving tickets? No accidents? Nothing? Ever?"

I hold my breath. If Sir Little answers, yes, it will be another nail in the prosecution's case.

"No. Never. I'm a careful driver."

Uncle Jasper stares hard at the knight. "No more questions at this time." He walks back to his chair.

I see him draw a beer stein and then cross it out with his pencil. Suddenly, he raises his hand, "Your honor, I would like to make a motion that all charges against my client be dismissed for lack of evidence."

Goode is on his feet. "Are you kidding? We haven't even started to present our evidence. Your honor, we have witnesses who saw the dragon leave the scene of the accident. We have a knight almost completely covered in bandages because he was so badly hurt and then left to die. We have—"

Judge Wolf pounds his gavel. "Mr. Doofinch, as much as I might agree, Mr. Goode says there's more evidence to see." He gives his head a shake. "I hate to waste costly court time, but your client is accused of a serious crime. So, before I can address your plea, more witnesses I want to see."

Goode smiles slyly. "I call Robin of Locksley."

"Oh good, he's calling Robin Hood," Uncle Jasper mumbles, an unhappy look on his face.

"You're rhyming," I hiss.

He sighs. "Goode calling Robin Hood, for their side, isn't so good." He gives me an upset look. "How's that for a rhyme?"

I'm not sure which is worse, Goode calling Robin Hood or my uncle's awful rhyme. Looking at Goode's sly smile, I suspect the answer.

CHAPTER 19

Robin Hood, tall and slender as a bow, dressed in his forest green suit and red cape, walks with confidence toward the witness stand. He takes his oath without hesitation, and when asked, proudly announces he is the Sheriff of Monstrovia. Every woman in the gallery, including the giants, and I suspect, Emily, are staring at his handsome features. He is a legend, a symbol of truth and bravery. The only problem: he's a witness for the other side.

Goode smiles at Hood. "Were you the officer in charge during the arrest of the defendant, Horace, that dragon?"

Robin loses his smile. "I was in charge of the arresting unit. Yes, sir."

"How many men were in that unit for this arrest?"

"A dozen, sir," Robin replies.

"Twelve men for one arrest?"

"We were arresting a dragon," Robin says.

"Did the defendant go peacefully?"

"The dragon didn't understand—"

"Please just answer the question?" Goode looks a bit annoyed.

"In the end, yes." Robin sucks in his lips.

"Not in the beginning?"

Goode is using the same trick as my uncle: using the witness's own words to frame new questions.

"No, not in the beginning."

Uncle Jasper stands. "For the sake of time, and out of respect for Sheriff Hood, the defense will agree that in the beginning, Horace did not go willingly

69

because he felt frightened. How would you feel if twelve knights woke you from a sound sleep?"

"Thank you, Mr. Doofinch," Goode says. "You bring me to my next question. Sheriff Hood, Mr. Doofinch claims Horace was frightened. What was he so afraid of?"

"Objection!"

"Sustained. Mr. Goode, there is no way Mr. Hood can know why Horace was frightened unless he can read the dragon's mind." Judge Wolf smiles at Robin. "Not even a legend, such as Mr. Hood, can do that. Now, can he?"

"If he could find the dragon's mind," a knight says, and there is laughter in the gallery.

Judge Wolf hits his gavel once, and the laughter subsides.

Goode nods. "Let me try it another way. How did the dragon react when you tried to arrest him?"

"He became upset."

"That's all? Did he try to resist arrest? Did he use a weapon?"

"He tried to burn our butts," a knight shouts and clamps his fist over his mouth.

"Objection! My client is not on trial for resisting arrest." Uncle Jasper says.

Wolf looks at Goode. "Why is that, Mr. Goode? Why isn't he charged with resisting arrest if he tried to burn their butts?"

Goode smiles slyly. "Because the sheriff didn't press charges, your honor."

Judge Wolf looks at Robin. "I see. That's a mystery."

Goode replies. "The sheriff didn't want to testify today, but as the arresting officer, had to obey my order."

"That's good for our side," I whisper to uncle Jasper.

Uncle Jasper nods. "Maybe."

Wolf studies Robin and says, "Mr. Hood, I expect honesty from you. Please, be sure what you say is true?"

Robin nods. "I always do, sir. Whether I like the accused or not, as an officer sworn to uphold the law, I always tell the truth."

Goode circles closer. "Did Horace try to burn their butts?"

"Objection. How can this witness know what Horace tried to do?"

"Sustained," Judge Wolf says.

Goode stops to think. "What weapon did the defendant use to resist arrest?"

Robin shifts in his seat. "He was building up a fireball, but—"

"A fireball? Isn't that terribly dangerous?"

The judge shakes his head and says, "Mr. Goode, we all know the danger of dragonfire. Please, get to the point that you aspire?"

Goode nods and asks, "Did the dragon shoot out the fireball?"

Robin Hood glances at the cage with Horace looking at him with sad eyes. "Yes, but he aimed it so—"

"Please, just a yes or no answer? Did the dragon shoot out the fireball? Yes or no?"

Robin Hood sighs. "Yes."

"But it didn't hit anyone. Is that correct? Yes or no?"

"Yes. I mean, no, it didn't hit anyone."

"Do you see the boy seated next to Mr. Doofinch?"

Why is he bringing me into this?

"I do."

"Was he present when you attempted to arrest Horace?"

"Yes."

"Did you report that he stopped the dragon from firing the fireball at you?"

Robin smiles at me. "Yes, I did."

"So, it was this boy who stopped the dragon from killing you?"

Robin exhales a blast of air. "Yes. He's a brave lad."

I feel proud when he says that, but Goode doesn't give me much time to enjoy it.

"Otherwise, you and your twelve brave knights might have been burnt to death by the defendant. Isn't that correct?"

Robin sighs again. "Yes, but—"

"Yes or no?"

"Yes."

Goode walks over to his table and picks up a sheet of paper. "Is this your arrest report?" He hands it to Robin.

"Yes. I recognize my signature."

"Can you read the line numbered 7 on page 1 of your sworn report?"

Robin smiles nervously. "The charge listed is "hit-and-run with grievous injuries, a possible fatality." Is that the line you wanted me to read?"

"Yes. Is this your handwriting?"

"Yes, I wrote it."

"So, the warrant was for leaving the scene of a possibly fatal accident?"

"Yes."

"Did you witness the accident?"

"No. Officer B. A. Dash was the first officer on the scene."

"And Officer B. A. Dash reported the "hit-and-run" to you?"

"Yes."

"And he called the ambulance?"

"Yes."

"Objection! Your honor, wouldn't the best evidence be from Officer Dash?"

Judge Wolf replied, "I agree. It would be best if Dash was your next witness."

"Thank you, your honor, I plan to call Officer B.A. Dash as my next witness." He turns back to the sheriff. "Mr. Hood, you are a knight, aren't you?"

"Yes. I am a member of the Monstrovian Loyal Order of Knights."

"Are you a Dragonslayer?"

"No. I'm not."

"Aren't all knights sworn to kill dragons?"

"No, we're not."

"So, it isn't true then that all knights want to kill dragons?"

Robin faces the audience. "No, Mr. Goode. Most knights are not members of the secret society of Dragonslayers. That's as big a myth as believing all dragons are man-killers. Just as I believe there are good dragons and bad ones, there are good knights too."

"I believe that too, Sheriff Hood. Thank you."

Uncle Jasper stares at Robin Hood. He then studies the faces of the people in the gallery. Everyone is looking at Robin. They seem to love the legendary outlaw, now turned famous lawman. "I'm not sure I want to risk questioning him," he whispers. "Your honor, I would like to thank Mr. Hood for his help in this case and ask that I may be able to call him later.

"Are you sure, Uncle?" I ask.

"Mr. Hood, you may step down but do not leave town," Judge Wolf says, looking at my uncle as if he's crazy not to question this critical witness.

I think so too.

As Robin walks by our table, he's exactly how I picture a hero, tall and athletic, with a handsome face. All the women are leaning forward to catch a better look. He is the exact opposite of my uncle. Except for one thing, neither of them ever gives up. He looks down at my uncle and shakes his head. "I'm truly sorry."

"You are an honest man. I admire you," Uncle Jasper says.

"Your nephew is a brave boy," Robin says and leaves the room.

"What do you think?" I ask Uncle Jasper.

"Everyone liked him, and I don't blame them. He comes across as honest and brave. When he said it was a hit-and-run, nobody doubted it. I even believed him."

"Why didn't Robin press charges against Horace for resisting arrest?" Emily asks.

Uncle Jasper smiles at her. "I think because he understood why Horace did that."

"Wouldn't it help Horace if you asked Robin Hood that question?" I ask.

Uncle Jasper picks up a file and smiles at me. "I was going to, but the sheriff not pressing charges on a dragon resisting arrest could hurt us."

"How?" I ask.

"It makes him appear partial to dragons. That makes his testifying for the state even worse because he says the dragon did bad things even though he doesn't think dragons are bad."

"I don't get it."

Uncle Jasper looks as if he's thinking of how to explain. "Let's pretend there are two Robin Hoods. Robin A hates dragons, while Robin B likes them." He draws two Robins on his pad and puts a capital A in one, and a B in the other.

"I'm glad there aren't two Emilies," I joke.

"Nor two Brodies," Emily fires back.

Uncle Jasper shakes his head. "This is serious. Let's say both Robins say that Horace did a bad thing. Which one would you take more seriously?"

Emily nods. "I get it now. Because Robin A likes dragons, if he says Horace did something bad, it's much worse than if the Robin who hates dragons says it."

"So, that's why you didn't ask Robin any questions." I understand now too.

"Yes. I was afraid Goode might get Sheriff Hood to say something that would make it much worse for Horace because Robin is someone everyone respects as a good and honest man."

"So, what do we do next?" I ask.

Uncle Jasper places the files back into his case. He clamps the lock closed. "We go back over everything again. I know there's something we're missing. I just can't see it."

I see Goode posing for the pixie photographers. He's all smiles and waves. Why doesn't he look worried?

Emily taps my shoulder. "Brodie, what do you think Goode has up his sleeve?"

"I wish I knew. I wish I knew."

CHAPTER 20

U ncle Jasper's desk is always covered with folders, papers, and thick law books. I've seen him sit here for hours, going over all the endless pages of witness interviews and court records. I love solving mysteries, so I don't mind some research, but sometimes reading all these forms and papers can be really BORING. It's like climbing a mountain but never reaching the top.

"I need you to do something for me, Brodie. Go to the Brain Room and get me information about this Officer B. Alder Dash. He's scheduled to be Goode's next witness. I want to know everything you can find out about him."

"The Brain Room?" I hate my uncle's computer. Strange things always happen when I use it.

"Take Silas with you. If he's not busy with one of Mavis's chores?" He chuckles, "Poor man."

I nod but have no intention of inviting Silas to help me with the Brain. He's crazier than that thing even. "What are you going to do?" I ask.

"I wish I knew. I think I'm going to go back over everything one more time. I know there's something I'm missing." He buries himself in his files.

I reluctantly head to the Brain Room. For once, it is quiet in the dark cavern that separates our living quarters from his offices in the mansion. The ceiling is high, and the floor is muddy, so his clients don't hurt their feet. Think about that. It's really a strange house.

When I get to the other side of the hall, I see the sign warning, "STAY OUT!" In pencil, Silas added, "Except for Brodie." It's still not in paint, reminding me

THE CASE OF THE KILLER KNIGHTS

that my stay here was supposed to be temporary. Even after a year, I'm still not sure I want to stay in Monstrovia. Yes, I like my uncle, Silas, even Mavis, and Horace. I just don't know if I can ever feel comfortable with all the other 'residents' here. And I still miss Mom and Dad. If one of them showed up, I don't know what I'd do. "Would I stay here or go home?" I let slip as I try to tip-toe silently across the dirt floor of the hallway, so I don't wake the...

Just as I feared. The echo shouts, "Go home...home...home."

I hate that echo. He twists everything I say. "I'm not leaving," I shout back.

"You should leave...leave...leave," the echo replies and adds, "Nobody wants you here...nobody...nobody...nobody."

That hurts. I'd answer that rotten echo, but I have no time to argue now. I pull open the door to the Brain Room.

The light from a three-headed dragon ceiling lamp comes on.

I plunk myself into a chair and stare at the blank screen, hesitating. There's no power button on Uncle Jasper's state-of-the-art computer. It's controlled by focusing thoughts. Sounds great, but that's how I almost got eaten by a serpent the first time I used this Brain. I've got to be careful not to think of anything dangerous.

The screen glows.

I'm ready. Focus. Focus.

The screen flashes. A cloud in the center shapes into a large building. Silas taught me how to maneuver through buildings with an avatar that looks like me. Where can I find the personnel files of police officers? My avatar races through the halls of the large building, but the screen fades. I try to concentrate. No good. I guess I'm tired.

"You're too tired for what?" A voice asks.

"Oh, no. It's a mistake. I didn't mean to call you."

"Oh, I see. You call me, and it's a mistake? Very nice."

"Emily, I have work to do." I cringe at her smiling face. I think there are more freckles on Hologram Emily than even on the real Emily, but I never counted. I guess I like freckles, which is why my imagination gave this Emily so many.

"So, what's your question?" Emily asks, her eyes greener than I remember.

"What makes you think I have a question?"

"You only call me when you want something. So what is it?" Emily's arms are crossed over her chest.

"I don't want anything. I told you, it was a mistake."

"There are no mistakes. You do want something, but your dopey brain doesn't want to admit it."

"I don't want anything. Now, leave me alone so I can get my work done."

Emily wags her finger at me. "The last time you let your mind wander, you almost got eaten by something your imagination cooked up. Do you remember that, or do you want me to show you?"

"No! I remember."

"Well, then?"

"Okay. I need to find records of a police officer named, B. Alder Dash."

"That's easy-peasy. Go to the Hall of Records."

"I tried that already. I couldn't find the right room."

"Boys," Emily mutters and then smiles. "That's why you need us girls around."

"Emily, I don't have time for arguing with you right now. Can you please help me find the right office?"

The screen flashes. A larger building appears dead center and spreading from one side of the monitor to the other. And standing right in front is Emily. "Go in this door and look for the 'Human Resources' room." She smiles and looks like she's waiting for something. "Don't you have something to say?"

"Thank you," I say, hoping it's the magic phrase that will make her disappear.

"Thank you for what?" She looks impatient. "Thank you, Emily, for helping me. Is that so hard to figure out?"

"Thank you, Emily, for helping me."

"You're welcome, Brodie." She smiles again. "Don't forget, you want the 'Human Resources' office."

"I won't." Thank goodness, she's finally gone. But now I see a pair of bear-head guards blocking the doorway of the building. I know it's my fear that created them, but they're still scary.

"Human! What is you doing here?" A guard says, advancing toward me until his face fills the entire screen. "I hate humans," he growls, his teeth are now all I see across the entire screen.

I pull away and close my eyes.

When I open them, I don't see Bear-head or his teeth. "I did it! I controlled him!"

"You controlled who, human?"

The bear's arm is half-way through the screen.

He's coming for me! "Emily, where are you when I need you?"

CHAPTER 21

What would you do if you saw a big, hairy, bear claw with sharp nails poking out of a computer monitor, reaching for you?

"RUN! RUN! RUN!"

I tell that to my brain, and the next thing I know is I see myself on the screen in cherry-red shorts and a sleeveless racing top, running on a track. I'm like a cartoon character, my legs moving like airplane propellers. I hardly touch the ground. I look back and no bear. "Wow! Great! I'm safe."

"Grrrr!"

What's that? I turn around and guess what's running after me? Not one! Not two! Three bears in shorts, tees, and gigundo sneakers! And they're gaining on me!

"Halt human!"

I know this isn't real, but it sure feels like it is. I can even feel the bear hot breath getting close. Closer. Too close!

"We got you now!" A bear shouts.

"They're not real!" I slam to a stop, turn around, raise my arms, and let out the biggest growl ever! "GRRRRRR!"

They're gone. I'm safe.

All I have to do now is figure out some way to stop running.

I close my eyes and think hard.

I'm back at the government building. This time, I keep myself from worrying about guards, and I don't see even one. I'm in control!

I'm in a hallway. It's lined with lots of doors. I search for one that says, 'Human Resources,' just like Emily said. "Whammo!" There it is! I pull open the door and stare in horror at an endless room lined with thousands of file cabinets. "I'll never find it." Suddenly I hear a strange noise.

I back away, but it's too late. The drawers are all sliding open.

"No!"

Papers are flying out in all directions.

I duck as a notebook comes flying through the computer screen.

As I stare in terror, hiding under the computer table, the Brain Room fills up with sheets of paper flying everywhere.

Someone is laughing.

I'm trying to focus, to end this nightmare, but I can't get control. I know that I imagine all this, but I can't stop it. "I hate paperwork!" I shout, and the papers become even more violent.

There's that laughter again.

I duck a barrage of books smashing their way into the room. "Stop! Stop!" I scream as the books and papers are mounting up all around me. I'm going to drown! I can't even get out from under the desk.

There are books everywhere. I close my eyes, too tired to focus, letting the computer do what it wants with me. I can't fight it. Can't concentrate. My eyes close.

"You always hated books," a voice cackles, and bursts into rude laughter.

It's true. I hate books, and now I'm drowning in them. Principal Feeney will laugh when he hears how I was killed by tons of books and papers. "I love books," I shout. "Do you hear? I love books!"

Laughter again?

"What's that?" I see something crawling over the mountain of books.

"I keeps tellin' ye' yer human boy brain is too scattered fer this computer," Silas Bumbernickle says as he shakes me awake. "What was ye doin' in here? Ye' coulda' been suffocated by all this mess I cleaned up fer ye.' What was ye thinkin' about, me best friend in the whole world?"

"Stop shaking me!" I push his hand away. "I guess I fell asleep," I mumble, looking around and seeing the papers and books are nowhere in sight.

Silas glares down at me. "This contraption is dangerous if ye can't stay in control. Now, tell me what ye was huntin' fer?"

"My uncle sent me to find the records of a policeman." I search my brain. "His name...his name? Officer Baldric Alder Dash."

"Who?"

"It's to help Horace."

"Well, why didn't ye say so?"

I'm still trying to shake myself awake when I see Silas has scrunched up his eyebrows, thick as caterpillars, and is staring, as if hypnotized, at the monitor. "Ye' has to focus."

A building appears. "I was in this building before."

"What room does ye need?" Silas is racing through the hallway.

"Human Resources," I reply, still dazed from the paper attack.

"What did ye say?"

"Human Resources."

"Human? Here? In Monstrovia?" Silas bursts into loud laughter. "Brodie, ye knows you humans are a tiny minority here. There isn't no Human Resources office anywhere in Monstrovia."

"But Emily—"

Silas shakes his head. "Oh, now, I see. You was unable to focus clear because you was thinkin' of Miss Beanstalk again." He waggles a finger at me. "Ain't you learned nothin' from me? Can't ye see how I lose me focus whenever me lovely Mavis appears? It's only natural that you can't concentrate when your girlfriend—"

"She's not my girlfriend!" I feel like clobbering him, but he's helping me. "Can you please help me find this guy's records?" *No Human Resources? Duh. Wait until I talk to that Emily again! Hologram Emily? This is too confusing. But one of them played a dirty trick on me.*

"Let's try the Police Records." Silas zips his avatar through the hall and stops at the door, marked Police Records. "Ah, this be the office," he says, and instantly we're in a room with several rows of computers. "What's the name we needs again?"

"Officer Baldric Dash."

Silas focuses on the nearest computer in the room and the screen flashes. Almost instantly, a folder full of paper floats from an open file drawer and hovers in the air.

"Can you print it for me?" I'm still steaming about how Emily sent me to the non-existent Human Resources room. Unbelievable! How could I be fooled into thinking there would be a Human Resources room in Monstrovia, where everywhere you look, there are only inhuman creatures? Grrr! Emily!

The sound of a printer rattles away.

"While we're here, can you find any records for a knight named Sir Lance A. Little?"

"Is he a policeman?"

"Not that I know of."

"Then, we'll have to go to the LOOK." Silas replies, looking doubtful.

"What's that?"

"LOOK is the Loyal Order Of Knights." He shakes his head. "That's a bit too dangerous fer me. What is it yer lookin fer?"

"I don't know. Sir Little is the knight who was almost killed by Horace. I'm just trying to help."

Silas looks thoughtful. "Let's first get these papers and see if there's anything here that can help."

A huge pile of papers comes floating out of the computer screen.

"Is that all about Officer Dash?"

Silas nods. "The police keeps very complete records."

I'm weighed down by books and sheets of paper. "I'll never get through all this."

Silas checks his pocket watch and then reaches for a stack of files. "I'm not one for readin' such things, but fer me best friend in the whole world…" He searches his jacket pocket and pulls out a pair of round, wire-framed glasses.

"You wear glasses?"

"Only when I reads and drives," Silas says, looking a bit embarrassed. "I don't much like wearin' them though, makes me look like a leprechaun, don't ye know?"

And here I thought he was just a lousy driver! I promise myself I'll have a talk with him about wearing his glasses when he drives, but not right now. I have work to do if I want to help Uncle Jasper win this case. But I will definitely talk to him! Sheesh!

CHAPTER 22

"Isn't that now the strangest thing?" Silas mutters after nearly an hour of reading these endless reports.

"You found something?" I'm getting tired of all these boring pages. Nothing seems out of the ordinary.

Silas removes his glasses and rubs his nose. He slides a pile of papers in front of me. "Look at item 3, page one, and 273, page 3."

I'm so tired my eyes are crossing. I look anyway. "They're crime and emergency call reports." I look at Silas. "Did you read every one of these? There must be thousands!"

"I skimmed the lot. But look at 3 and 273."

I run my finger from the top of the first page and find entry number 3: "Crash report. Zig-Zag Highway, Tier 6, turn 9. Victim knocked to the ground with multiple injuries by an unknown assailant." So what?"

"Now, look at the end of the entry."

""Baldric A. Dash." I still don't get the problem."

"Ye' must be tired. Look at number 273."

"Crash report. Zig-Zag Highway, Tier 6, Turn 9. Victim knocked to the ground with multiple injuries by an unknown assailant." I look at Silas. "That is odd. It's the exact same report." I rush to the end of the entry. "Baldric A. Dash." I race back to the first page, then back to page 3. A flicker of hope. "Are there a lot more like this?"

"None. I just thought it was strange seein' two the exact same."

I run down a few dozen entries, stopping when I find the word, 'crash.' None of them matches item 3 and 273. I let out a loud yawn. "It's a wild goose chase. Good try."

"I best be goin' now," Silas says. "Sorry I couldn't find nothin' fer ye." He gets up and walks to the door. "Ye know, I never realized until late how much that big firebreather means to me." He scratches his butt. "Ain't that always the way? Ye never knows what someone means to ye' until ye loses them."

"We're not going to lose Horace. Uncle Jasper won't let that happen."

Silas nods, but he looks sad as if he doesn't really believe me.

I glance at the pile of papers, wishing I could make them disappear. "I'll stay and finish this."

Silas gives me a smile. "Yer like yer uncle. He never sleeps neither when he has work to do. But you're a growin' lad and needs yer sleep. Come on then, and ye'll be fresh as a butterfly in the morn."

I know he's right, so I pick up the stack of papers and head up the three flights of stairs to my room. I like living in the attic. I feel safe from some of my uncle's more scary clients. One night, he even had a vampire visit him. I remember I hardly could sleep, especially when Perry Mason's eyes were staring down at me—they looked like the vampire's eyes.

I look at the posters of the great fictional lawyer my uncle had hung all around my room and place the papers under his gigantic face. "Maybe you can see something I'm missing," I mutter, and barely make it to my bed.

I crawl under the covers. I'm exhausted, but every time I close my eyes, I see Horace's sad face. I hear a scratchy sound. Someone is looking down at me from the attic rafter. I peer into the shadows and see two red eyes, blood-red. "Vake up, boy," a voice hisses, sounding like steam from a teapot.

"Who are you?" I crawl to a corner of my bed. "What do you vant...want?" I ask, straining to see the shape of this creature lurking in the rafters.

"Ve vant you," the voice says.

"Who's ve?"

"I am," another voice says.

I jump at the sight of a mummy inches away from me. He's all wrapped in bandages.

"Who are you?" I pull the blanket over me.

"You know who I am," the mummy says. "Your dragon did this to me, and now I'm going to do it to you."

I jump out of bed, fists raised.

"You can't fight us, boy," the mummy says and pulls my legs out from under me.

I'm flat on my back on my blanket, staring up at the ceiling.

The red-eyed creature drops slowly down a blood-red string toward me. It's a giant spider, but it has Goode's face, strong mandibles opening and snapping shut.

"Leave me alone? Leave me alone?" I kick my legs, but the mummified knight is holding my ankles. Why can't I move my arms? I look up and see two hairy paws clamped down on my wrists. A little higher up, I see the sharpest white teeth I've ever seen.

"Don't move. Don't try anything. If you scream, you will die."

"Judge Wolf? You're in on this too?" I don't know which is worse, his breath or his rhymes.

"Your uncle has been very bad, so you must pay, my poor, little lad." He bares his teeth and a drop of spittle sizzles on my forehead.

I try to wriggle free, but the spider is now an inch above my face. His eyes paralyze me. Hairy spider jaws aimed to clamp down on my flesh.

Suddenly, the spider with Goode's face speaks, "If you want to live, call your uncle. Tell him to come up to your room. If not..." He shoots a glance at the mummy.

The Mummy holds a large roll of bandages in his clawed hand. "First, my spider friend will bite your throat. It will be only a small bite, but you will feel numb at first, then be paralyzed. But don't worry. You'll be able to see and feel everything we are doing to you."

That doesn't sound like something to not worry about.

The Mummy pulls a bandage from his mouth. "That's better. Then, I will wrap you in these bandages. I'll start with your toes, then work up ever-so-slowly to your shins, your knees, thighs...then your hands and arms...all wrapped up, tight. The final wrapped gift will be your head—"

"But he must see, his final destiny," Wolf says. "I want to see the shivering fear and painful surprise in his terrified eyes."

Goode laughs. "We'll teach your uncle a lesson he won't forget. He thinks he can defeat me again. Not this time."

"He's just doing his job," I say, unable to break free.

Wolf's saliva drips down into my eye. "Once all wrapped, you will burn. Then your uncle, his lesson will learn." He lights a long match and bursts into shrill laughter. "Fire! Fire! Burning bright. We'll watch you burn with delight. Oh, the pain and the joy as we fricassee your uncle's boy."

The spider's legs are on my nose. I wriggle it to throw 'Hairy' off. He tickles. But then I see his jaw open, and a pointy tongue slithers from his mouth. I feel a sharp pain in my cheek. "Objection! Objection!" It's my last scream as my body grows numb. "I ob….ject…"

"Objection overruled!"

Who said that? Whose voice is that? I recognize her voice. Emily? "Ettu Emily? Not you too?" I see her leering, freckled face, but her teeth are those of a vampire.

I let out a terrified scream and wake up. I'm in a sweat, heart pounding. I can't move. What the heck did I dream? I know it was awful, but I can't remember most of it. I do remember the hairy spider, the salivating mummy, Judge Wolf…Emily. They wanted my uncle to stop hurting Sir Little. I'm still shaking. Do I try to stop him? Will that end the nightmare?

I get dressed, still unsteady. Fully clothed, I see what looks like a hint of a smile on the Perry Mason poster's lips. It must be the sun's reflections through the blinds.

I walk over to the framed poster. No smile. Mason never smiles.

Several piles of paper are lying on the floor. How did they get there? Was the window open? I peer up at the rafters. No spider. No red eyes. The window is locked shut. What knocked the papers over?

I walk back and pick them up. I set the pile on top of the stack still on my bookcase when my eye hits on the first entry on the top page. It's titled, #2,097: Crash report. It's probably nothing, but I read on: "Zig-Zag Highway. Tier 6. Turn 9." I race to the end of the report. "Darn!" It's not signed by Officer Dash, but initialed, B.A.D. Too bad. So much for that hunch.

I look at the Mason poster. He's as stern-looking as ever, staring at me with those dark, penetrating eyes. "Why can't I have a poster of a girl band in here? Why are you still looking at me?" I'm about to leave the room, but that darn poster keeps me from going. "What do you want from me? I tried my best." Was it? Did I miss something too?

I glance at entry #2,097 again. Just to please Mason. "Victim knocked to the ground with multiple injuries." It sounds exactly the same. Coincidence? I skip to the end of the entry and see the reporting officer signed it as B.A.D. "I'm done! It's hopeless!" I slam the file closed and throw it on my bed. "Perry Mason or not, I'm outa here!" And just like that, it hits me. "B.A.D.?" Can it be this obvious?

I race to my bed, grab the folder, and flip the pages to entry 3. I then return to #273, and finally back to #2,097. I glare at Mason. "Oh, fine! You're such a darn know-it-all!" I grab a stack of the boring reports and throw myself on the bed, a yellow highlighter in my hand. I know it's a long-shot, but I've got to try. Mason's making me do it. Nightmare or not, I'm going to help my uncle win this case.

CHAPTER 23

I'm still going through the files, half-asleep, when Mavis calls, "Brodie, yer gonna miss yer uncle and the court!"

I should go back to bed. I'm too excited. I find my uncle at his desk. He looks like he hasn't slept either. "I think I found something," I tell him, placing the pile of papers on his desk.

"I hope so. I'm totally befuddled with this case." He reaches for the papers. "You used a highlighter?"

"What do you think?" I ask, as nervous as when I hand in a test to my teachers.

Uncle Jasper flips through the pages. "No. No. No. No." He turns back to the first page. "No. I don't know. Hmmm?" He looks up at me and then dives back into the file again.

"So, what do you think?" I'm leaning across the table, on pins and needles, waiting.

He suddenly grabs his phone. "Good morning, Emily. I need you to do something for me. It's for Horace."

Emily? Why is he calling her? I'm the one who did all the work!

"Come, Brodie, we're late." Uncle Jasper darts out of the office carrying his case in one hand and the stack of papers I gave him in the other. "Grab the door," he bellows.

We charge past Mavis and out the front door to where Silas is waiting with his mushroom-shaped cab.

"We're late," Uncle Jasper says, hopping into the front seat of the cab. "Hurry, Brodie, I haven't all day."

My uncle hasn't said a word about my work. I hardly slept finishing it, and he hasn't said so much as a thank you. I slump in the back seat and pull the shoulder harness around me. "Why don't you put on your glasses?" I urge Silas before he has a chance to step on the gas.

"I didn't know you wear glasses?" Uncle Jasper says. "That could explain a few things."

Silas digs out the wire-framed glasses and places them on his nose. "Do I look like a leprechaun?" He asks.

"Yes!" I reply, hoping the glasses make him a better driver.

"Ye see. I told ye so." He sighs. "Shall I rocket?"

Uncle Jasper looks at me. "No. One of us looks like he had a busy night."

I want to yell at Uncle Jasper, that to save his skin…that's why I look so tired, but I can't keep my eyes open. I also don't want to talk to him in case I blurt out how angry I am that he gave my work to Emily, and never thanked me for what I did.

"Brodie. Brodie." Uncle Jasper says, "Maybe you should go home with Silas. You're exhausted—"

I force myself to sit up. "I'm fine." I'm not. I'm tired and steaming mad.

"Well, then we'd best hurry up, or we'll be late." Uncle Jasper shakes his head. "Okay, Mr. Bumbernickle, rocket!"

Silas becomes a rocket pilot again, and that's enough to wake me up. He zigs and zags through the lines of weird vehicles that race across the multiple tiers of the Zig-Zag Highway. Even with the harness on, I'm thrown all over the seat, but that's not what's bothering me. Uncle Jasper is still reading through the files I highlighted for him. "I hope Emily can work a miracle," he says, giving me a smile.

I'm staring at the alien creatures piloting their crafts helter-skelter on this multi-tiered highway. Horns are blaring, and everyone is racing around in odd-ball speeders bouncing in the road's loops and dips. It's like a roller coaster, but not on one track. I'll never be able to drive here. My head is throbbing.

"Faster, Silas," My uncle says.

I don't have time to protest, because Silas slams on the brakes and we're at the Giant Courthouse. "Thanks for the ride," I say, thinking the glasses didn't help at all.

"Ye'll get yer land legs in a coupla' dragon-swallows," the mad driver says and speeds away, leaving a cloud of dust behind him.

I race to catch up with Uncle Jasper, but as usual, he's way ahead of me. And there are the bear-headed guards. I know they're going to stop me. I prepare to argue with the guards when I hear Uncle Jasper say, "He's with me. He's my brilliant assistant." He pats me on the back and announces, "He solved my case."

I'm surprised and relieved the guards let me through with just a quick pass under the metal detector. "Thank you," I say, feeling a bit better. "Have a nice day." Did I really say that to these human-haters?

One guard grunts, but the other gives me a nod and what looks like a smile. That's an improvement, I think, as I rush with my uncle up the elevator and onto the moving belt that takes us to the courtroom.

"We're just in time," Uncle Jasper says, throwing his briefcase on the table. "You did well, my boy. I would have left you home to finish but want you here with me while Emily does the research." He places his hand on my shoulder. "You are more perceptive. You see things that even I sometimes miss."

I'm beaming as I sit down and pull out my legal pad, while he digs out various folders from his battered case. A shadow over us makes me look up.

"I wasn't sure you were going to make it," Goode says, blasting us with his perfect teeth.

"Did anyone ever say you look like Perry Mason?" I ask, startled by the resemblance.

Goode looks puzzled. "Is he some handsome actor from your human sector?"

I look at my uncle, and he smiles.

Goode shakes his head. "I'll never understand humans."

The court becomes silent as Judge Wolf enters. He looks surly already, his gray furry facial hair needs to be brushed flat. "Let's get this case done. Call witness number one," he says to Goode.

"I call Officer Baldric Dash," Goode announces.

"Oh, no." I gasp and clap my hands over my mouth. My uncle warned me a hundred times not to show any emotions or reactions, and I just did.

"Oh yes," Goode says, grinning ear to ear, after overhearing me.

Uncle Jasper shoots me a look that could fry dragon eggs.

CHAPTER 24

I imagine Emily leaning over, her fingers digging into my arm. "You know you're not supposed to show any reaction," she says.

She's such a miss know-it-all, but once again, she's right. Even when she's not here. "Sorry, Uncle," I whisper.

"Shhh," he says and scoots forward in his chair.

"Call Officer Baldrick Alder Dash," the clerk shouts.

The officer enters and walks to the front of the courtroom.

A bear-head clerk stands before him with a copy of the United States Constitution in his paw. "Do you swear to tell the truth, the whole truth, and nothing but the truth according to the laws of Monstrovia and the Constitution of the United States of America?"

"I do," Dash says.

"You may be seated," the clerk says and walks back to his desk.

Officer Dash, a tall man in a policeman's blue uniform, takes the stand.

Goode approaches. "Thank you for being here, Officer Dash. We appreciate your valiant service as an enforcer of our laws."

The officer nods. "I'm always happy to do my duty."

Goode smiles, and so does the Judge. "You were the first officer on the scene of the alleged accident. Is that correct?"

Dash grimaces. "Yes. I was."

"And you filed the accident report?"

"I did."

Goode holds up a stapled bunch of papers. "Do you recognize this report?"

The officer examines the bottom of the three pages. "Yes. This is my report.

My signature is on each page."

"May I see the original report?" Uncle Jasper asks.

Goode signals his secretary, who delivers the papers to my uncle.

Uncle Jasper reads the top sheet, the second page, the third, and finally gets to the last page. "Your honor, the defense agrees that this is the original report."

The judge shakes his head. "Well, thank you for that."

Goode smiles. "Can you please read aloud what you wrote on line 22 of the first page?

"I'm sorry, your honor, what page and line?" Uncle Jasper looks confused. He sneezes and drops the papers. "Oh, I'm sorry." He bends over to pick them up and knocks more papers off the table.

The knights in the gallery snicker. Some mumble about my uncle's clumsiness. One calls him a bumbler.

"Mr. Doofinch! Are you ill?" The judge asks. "Or just clumsy?"

Goode walks over and hisses, "You're up to something? What's going on?"

"Will you two please hurry this along?" Judge Wolf checks his watch. "Wasting court time is costly and wrong."

Goode bares his teeth. "You'd better stop this, or I'll stop it for you."

"I have no idea what you mean," Uncle Jasper replies. "I'm sorry, your honor, what page and line was that again?"

The judge throws up his paws. "I have no idea! Mr. Goode?"

Goode walks back to the table. "What line was that?" He asks his secretary, who hands him a copy of the report. He hands it to my uncle.

"Your honor, I know it's a detail, but could you please ask Mr. Goode to use the original report, and not a copy? For the record."

"Mr. Goode, would you please use the original—you heard what he said." The Judge sounds annoyed. "One minute. Mr. Doofinch, if I find you are deliberately delaying this hearing, I will hold you in contempt. I never fail. You'll be in jail."

"Who me?" Uncle Jasper gives him the "who me?" look. I know that one well. I use it whenever I get into trouble. Is he in trouble? Is that what this delaying tactic is about?

Goode snarls, "May I please continue with this witness?" He holds up the original report. "Now, Officer Dash, will you read line 22, page one, of this ORIGINAL report?" He waves the original in front of my uncle and then hands the report to the amused officer.

Officer Dash finds the line and reads, "When I arrived on the scene, I did not see the driver who crashed into the grievously injured knight."

Goode nods. "In other words, the other driver was gone before you arrived?"

"Yes. The victim was lying on the ground, crying in agony. I thought he was going to die."

"So, you called for help?"

"Yes. It was awful. I don't know how anyone could leave an accident victim like that."

"Objection! He should be directed to only answer yes or no."

Goode snarls, "He's my witness! I can have him answer any way I want!" He runs his hand through his black hair.

"I'll bet he uses shoe polish to make it look so black," I hiss.

Emily giggles.

My uncle signals me to be quiet.

The judge shakes his head. "Overruled. Mr. Goode is correct. It is his witness, and if he wants the Officer to give complete responses, that is his choice."

Goode frowns. "Can you read the last sentence on page 2?"

Uncle Jasper asks, "Page 2?"

"Yes. Page 2! The last sentence! Good grief!" Goode shakes his head angrily. "Officer Dash, would you mind reading the last sentence on page 2?"

Dash searches the page and reads, "An APB...that's 'all-points bulletin,' was posted for Horace Dragon, upon suspicion of leaving the scene of an accident resulting in grievous bodily injury."

Goode is smiling again. "Did the defendant ever return to the scene?"

"No. Not to my knowledge."

"Based on your years of experience, do you believe this was a 'hit-and-run' situation?"

"Objection!" Uncle Jasper calls out after eyeing the door at the back of the courtroom.

"Your objection astounds. Mr. Doofinch. On what grounds?" The judge asks, barely able to contain his annoyance.

"Mr. Goode is asking for an opinion?"

"I said, "based on his years of experience." That is asking for an expert opinion," Goode says. "He's an EXPERT, so I can ask for his opinion!"

"Oh, so you're saying this officer is an expert?" Uncle Jasper asks, glancing at the doors again.

"I certainly think he is, don't you?" Goode replies. "Are you really going to ask me to prove he is an expert at his job?"

"Not in my court he isn't," Judge Wolf barks. "This is not the day for another delay. Go on with your question. I'm getting indigestion."

Goode looks at his notes. "Oh, yes. Based on your years of experience, can you give me your EXPERT opinion on whether this was a hit-and-run incident?" He looks at my uncle.

Uncle Jasper shrugs.

Dash smiles. "Based on my nearly twenty years of experience, yes, my expert opinion is that this was a hit-and-run incident."

"Thank you, officer, for your service and EXPERT testimony." Goode turns to Uncle Jasper. "I think we're done."

Uncle Jasper turns to the judge. "Your honor, may we request a delay until after lunch?"

The judge looks furious but glances at the clock. "You can't finish this by lunchtime? Is that what you're saying? For a fast verdict, I was praying."

Uncle Jasper sighs and shrugs his shoulders. "I'm terribly sorry, but I have quite a few questions for the good officer and would prefer to ask them in one session."

"I'd like to keep going, your honor," Goode says. "My opponent is just stalling."

Judge Wolf growls and then says, "Fine. The Court is in recess until 2:00 p.m. today, but then you'd better be ready to cross-examine this witness without more delay."

96

"He's rhyming again," I mutter.

"Where is that girl?" Uncle Jasper rasps after everyone leaves.

"Maybe she got kidnapped," I joke.

"Brodie, that's not funny." He's watching the door like a cartoon cat waiting for a yellow canary.

I guess he's right. It isn't funny. "Sorry. I sometimes say dumb things when I'm nervous."

He gives me a smile. "I do too. Sometimes, when I'm not even nervous."

Even if he pretends he's not nervous, I can tell he is. If Emily doesn't show up soon, we'll run out of time. I glance at Horace, still poking his head out of the top of the cage. He looks sad. I wonder if he understands how hard we're all working to save him.

CHAPTER 25

I walk with my uncle in the hallway when I hear the clanking of armor. A group of knights surrounds us. There are five of them.

One knight places himself in my uncle's face. Would they dare do something in a courthouse?

"You're making our friend look bad, Doofinch," the knight says, his gloved hand resting on the handle of his sword.

Uncle Jasper looks like a midget next to these guys, but replies, "I'm just doing my job."

"Your job is to make us look bad?" Another knight asks, glaring at my uncle.

"His job is to make sure everyone gets a fair trial," I say, realizing I'm placing myself in big danger.

Uncle Jasper puts his hand on my shoulder. "My nephew is right. If you were in trouble, you'd want me doing for you exactly what I'm doing now. You'd want me to provide the best defense possible."

The first knight sneers. "But we're not low-life dragons. Is we boys?"

"No. We're knights," the others shout, tightening the circle around my uncle.

Panic. I'm ready to run for help. My uncle is about to become shish-ka-bob.

"Leave him alone," a voice says.

I recognize Robin Hood. But will he help against his fellow knights?

The knight moves to one side and stares at the former outlaw. "We're not working with you, right now, traitor! You don't deserve to be a knight, turning against our terribly wounded brother like you done."

Robin frowns. "If being one of you means I must choose between what is

98

right and doing wrong to protect an unworthy knight, then I gladly give up my membership in your order."

"No, Robin," Another knight says and steps beside the brave sheriff.

The first knight curls his lips and snarls. "Our brotherhood demands we protect each other."

Several knights shout, "Brothers, one and all! Never let a brother fall!"

The first knight moves toward Robin. "You're a traitor," he repeats.

I see the others, three armored men, standing with the loud-mouth knight. I want to run, but my legs are rubber, and Uncle Jasper is in danger. Where are the bear-head guards when you need them?

Robin pulls his cape to one side. "No brother should make another do wrong. Have you all forgotten your sacred oath to uphold the truth, help the weak, and always do what is right?"

I see the rebellious knight's hand reach for something hidden under his chest plate. "Knife!" I scream.

A stocky knight next to him grabs his arm and holds it tight. "Robin's right. This is a court of law. We must not fight here."

"Let go of my hand," the other knight orders.

The other knights step between this mutineer and Robin. One says, "Baldric, Robin is right. Whatever quarrel we have with this lawyer is not for the halls of justice. We can fix him later."

"You're turning against me too?" The one called Baldric breaks free and shoves the others aside. "So much for brotherhood," he shouts and storms off. "Lawyer, wait until there is nobody around to save you."

I wonder what the others will do now that their rebellious leader has left.

"Thank you, men," Robin says. "That is the second time Baldric has challenged me."

Uncle Jasper looks puzzled. "Baldric? Do you mean Baldric Dash?"

Robin nods. "Sir Baldric Dash."

Uncle Jasper looks stunned. "Officer Dash is a knight?"

I slap my hand against my forehead. "Wow! I never thought of that."

The other knights gather around us as Uncle Jasper fills Robin Hood in on our suspicions about Baldric Alder Dash.

"But you have no proof," Robin says. "Even a lout like Sir Dash is innocent until proven guilty."

"No. I don't have proof yet. But I sent Miss Beanstalk to get me the proof. Alas, she hasn't returned." Uncle Jasper sighs. "I'm afraid it will be too late by the time she gets here."

Robin calls to his men. "I need two volunteers."

Two knights step forward.

"Thank you," Robin says. "The girl that was seated with Sir Doofinch, Miss Beanstalk, mount up and see if you can find her. We need her here as fast as possible."

Uncle Jasper extends his hand to the sheriff. "Thank you. You are indeed, my brother."

Robin clasps my uncle's hand. "We believers in the law must always stand together. Come, let us get back to the court? My merry men will find her. Have faith, my friend." He gives me a smile and says, "Learn from your uncle, lad. He's a fine man, a hero."

I'm tongue-tied. The great Robin Hood called my uncle a hero. As I walk back into the courtroom, the look on Goode's face when he sees Robin Hood walking with his hand on my uncle's shoulder is whip cream on my sundae.

Unfortunately, it melts just like ice cream when Judge Wolf enters and growls, "Doofinch, enough of your fun. It's time justice is done."

"Oh boy, he's rhyming still," I whisper to my uncle.

Uncle Jasper shoots worried looks at the rear door. "This is bad. Very, very bad."

Officer Dash, back in his uniform, reenters the courtroom. He strolls in as if nothing happened during the break.

"I recall Officer Baldric Dash," Uncle Jasper says in a wheezy voice.

Dash marches to the witness stand with shoulders straight and head raised high, shooting a scornful look at my uncle as he passes by the defense table.

The clerk reminds the officer that he's still under oath.

"Finish your questions, I've indigestion," Judge Wolf says, making a prune-like face.

Uncle Jasper looks at Robin, who looks at the door and then shrugs his shoulders.

I'm looking for Emily too. What's taking her so long?

Uncle Jasper takes a few moments to study his notes. He clears his throat. "Officer Dash, how long have you been a police officer?"

Dash straightens his uniform. "Nearly twenty years of service to Monstrovia."

"And a knight?"

"Fifteen years and proud of it!" He beams at the gallery.

Several show victory signs with their armored fingers.

The judge raises his gavel, and the hands drop.

Uncle Jasper glances at the door and then asks, "And how long have you been a Dragonslayer?"

Goode jumps up. "How long? How long? How long? Your honor, the only thing taking long, much too long, is Doofinch here. He's delaying the trial."

"I'm trying to question the witness, your honor. The defense has the right to do whatever it takes to defend our client—"

Judge Wolf holds up his paw. "Doofinch, I'll give you a while to finish this trial. But no more delay or you will pay."

"Yes, your honor," Uncle Jasper says, glancing at the door again, and then down at his notes. "I forgot where I was."

The clerk reads, "Officer, how long have you been a Dragonslayer?"

Goode groans.

Uncle Jasper repeats, "Officer Dash, how long have you been a Dragonslayer?"

Dash sits up straighter. "I was honored to join seven years and four months ago."

"Very good. And have you ever slain a dragon?"

"Objection!" Goode shoots out of his seat.

The judge shakes his head. "Since killing is a crime, even dragon slaying, we can't force him to admit to that. Stop delaying. Sustained."

Uncle Jasper nods slowly and then asks, "Isn't it true that to join the Dragonslayers, one must kill a dragon?"

"No."

101

"So, how do you become a Dragonslayer?"

"Do I have to answer that?" Dash looks at Goode for help.

The Judge replies. "I see no reason why you shouldn't. Goode, did you neglect to object?"

"No objection, your honor," Goode says, looking at his assistant who shrugs her shoulders.

Goode didn't object. I don't like that. What's he up to?

Dash smiles and says, "You take an oath to protect all living creatures from these monsters."

Uncle Jasper looks uneasily at me.

I think he didn't get the answer he hoped for.

Uncle Jasper pauses and then smiles at me. "By monsters, you mean dragons?"

"Naturally. It's obvious."

"So, you believe dragons are monsters?" He casts a glance at Horace. "Do you hate dragons?"

"I don't love them…like you do. How can you defend such a vicious creature? You're a knight, aren't you? What's wrong with you?" Dash shakes his head in disgust.

"I'm not on the witness stand, so I don't have to answer," Uncle Jasper says, sneaking another peek at the door.

"I don't have to answer either," Dash says.

"Yes, you do," Judge Wolf barks. "If you do not, I'll hold you in contempt of court, and you'll spend a day or two in jail. And there won't be any bail!"

The officer nods his head. "Sorry, sir."

Just then, the door opens. I hear the clanking of armor. All eyes focus on two knights escorting Emily to the defense table.

"What's the meaning of this? I recognize this miss." The judge roars. "Doofinch, answer quick. Is this another of your tricks?"

I look at Emily. Does she have it? She'd better. That judge is baring all his wolfish teeth and leaning dangerously close to the edge of his desk.

CHAPTER 26

"Your honor, may I have a moment to confer with my associate?" Uncle Jasper asks the judge.

"Your associate arrived in a whirl, but Doofinch, she's just a girl?" Judge Wolf rhymes, his fist wrapped tight on the gavel.

"Your honor, Mr. Doofinch has been delaying this court far too long. Allowing him more time is simply wrong." Goode looks surprised that he just rhymed too.

"Please, your honor. The defendant deserves every opportunity to prove his innocence." Uncle Jasper says.

The judge lets out a deep sigh. "One last break is all I'll give. Your defendant must have every chance to get a fair trial and live. But my friend, Doofinch, get this through your head. Waste my time and the dragon's dead." He lets out a low, rumbling growl.

Uncle Jasper hurries over to Emily. "Well? Well?"

Emily doesn't answer. She's out of breath.

"You didn't get it?" I ask. "I knew Uncle Jasper should have sent me."

"You tried, dear girl. Thank you." Uncle Jasper sighs.

Emily whispers, "Brodie was right."

Uncle Jasper whirls around. "Really? Are you sure?"

"Take a look at it yourself." Emily hands Uncle Jasper a sheet of paper. "It took forever to go through all the records, and your 'Brain' kept coming up with holograms...well, anyway, it was difficult."

"What holograms?" I ask, seeing Emily looking strangely at me.

"Nothing," she replies and turns away.

Uncle Jasper is studying the sheet of paper. He leans over the table and compares the numbers to the files I'd gone through that Silas had handed me. "Yes, I think we have what we need." He turns to Emily. "Thank you. I knew you could do it."

Emily is beaming.

"What holograms?" I ask her, as Uncle Jasper lays out the sheet of paper and the file on Goode's table.

"It's nothing," Emily replies but looks like she's blushing.

I'm about to ask her about the holograms again, but I hear Goode instructing his secretary to examine the evidence. When she's done, she looks up at him with a worried expression on her face. I hear her mumble, "I'm sorry. I didn't know."

Goode lunges down at the papers and then sighs. "Doofinch, you must believe me, I had no idea."

Uncle Jasper picks up the files. "I do believe you. Despite our differences, I believe you would never do anything to support something as low as this."

Goode nods. "I truly had no idea. You may do what you need. I won't object."

Uncle Jasper extends his hand.

Goode hesitates and then buries it in his own.

Uncle Jasper says, "For the record, I don't count this as a win."

Goode shakes his head. "If you succeed, it's a win for justice. That's what counts. We sometimes forget that in the heat of battle."

"Are you two finished with your dance?" Judge Wolf's voice shatters the chatter in the room. "Can we please finish this? I don't want my dinner to miss."

Goode rises. "Your honor, the state, to save time, will accept the new evidence uncovered by Mr. Doofinch, and his staff."

Judge Wolf growls, "What evidence? I've seen nothing! You'd better make clear, what's going on here?"

Uncle Jasper stands next to Goode. "Your honor, if you allow me to question this witness, I believe this new evidence will reveal the truth."

"And you have no objection to this new detection?" Wolf aims his glare at

Goode.

"Both Doofinch, and I, are interested in seeing that justice is done, your honor." Goode sits down and glares at his secretary. "I'd like to know how you missed what a young girl and boy could find? We'll discuss that later."

Uncle Jasper approaches the bench.

"Officer Dash, please remember you are still under oath."

"I know that." Dash smiles confidently at the gallery of knights.

"Good. Then you know the penalty for perjury?"

"I ain't lying. Is that what you two is talking about?"

"Please, just answer the questions."

"Yes. I know the penalty for perjury, but I'm not lying."

"Good. Now, let's get right to the accident. You were the first on the scene. Is that right?"

"Yes. I said that already."

"Where were you just before you got to the scene?"

"I was riding in my patrol car."

"And you got the call on your radio?"

"Yes."

"So how long from the time you got the call to when you got to the scene of the accident?"

"Not very long. I don't know."

"You don't know?" Uncle Jasper casts a skeptical look at the gallery.

"Not very long. Maybe five or ten minutes."

"So, you didn't arrive in time to see the defendant fly off?"

"Yes." The knight looks anxious. "No. I guess not."

"But in your accident report, you said you saw the defendant flying away from the accident scene?"

"I guess, yes, I saw him in the distance."

"How far away was he?"

"I don't know. Pretty far, I guess."

"So, you couldn't have seen his face?"

A knight shouts out, "You don't have to see his face to know he's a dragon! What a joke!"

"Order in the court!" Judge Wolf snaps at the knight. "You be quiet in the rear, or I'll throw you and your buddies out of here."

Uncle Jasper smiles. "Actually, the knight is correct. You don't have to see the face to know it's a dragon, do you, Sir Dash?"

Dash looks a little nervous, sweat now dripping down his face. But can my uncle nail him? If Dash did what I think he did, he just might get away with it. He's that sneaky.

I look at Emily, and she gives me that strange smile. On her pad, she's drawn a picture of a young man in a suit with sneakers on his feet...

Oh, no. Is that me?

CHAPTER 27

"Brodie, pay attention. I need you to observe the witness," Uncle Jasper rasps. I feel like telling him it's Emily causing the problem, but he's back up front with a bunch of cardboard posters. "You said, it was a dragon, but you didn't need the face to identify which dragon. Is that correct, Sir Dash?"

"I don't know what you mean? And it's, 'Officer,' not, 'Sir,' when I'm in uniform."

"My mistake. We'll come to that later." Uncle Jasper smiles warmly. "It's simple, Officer. If you saw a dragon from a distance, as you say, how did you know it was the defendant?"

"I still don't get it."

Uncle Jasper signals Emily and me. We get out of our seats and take the large photos from him. "My assistants are holding four photos of dragons. I want you to say 'stop' when they are about the distance you claim you were from the dragon who allegedly caused the accident."

Wolf shakes his head. "If this is another trick, you'd better get it done mighty quick."

Emily and I start walking to the rear of the courtroom.

"How do I know how far he was? I just know it was him." The officer sounds upset. "Okay. Stop! Stop!"

He stops us about two rows from the back of the twenty-row gallery.

Uncle Jasper walks next to Dash. "Is that about how far you'd say the dragon was?"

"I don't know. Yeah, I guess. He could have been farther, but that looks about right."

Uncle Jasper waves his hand. "Can you pick out which of the photos my assistants are holding is Horace?"

Emily and I hold up our large photos.

The witness leans forward atop the wooden railing of the witness box. He studies Horace in his cage and then focuses on the photos. His eyes are narrow as he goes from one photo to the other. "It's the one in the girl's right hand," he finally says.

Darn! It's the correct photo. I try not to show disappointment, but this is bad. I wonder how my uncle is going to react. This isn't what he wanted. He wanted him to pick the wrong picture.

Uncle Jasper remains silent, looking straight at the photo.

"Am I right?" The officer asks, still leaning forward.

Uncle Jasper asks quietly, "You're not sure?"

Uncle Jasper has told me many times, it's a good idea to sometimes remain silent, to wait and see what a witness will say if you wait long enough. As usual, he's right.

The officer looks hard again. "Yeah. I think it's him."

"Think? You're not one hundred percent sure?"

"It's hard to tell from this distance."

"But, you said you could have been even farther away."

"Yeah, but a dragon is much larger than those dopy cards."

Uncle Jasper signals us to bring the cards back to our table.

"Did I get it right?" Officer Dash asks again. "Judge, he isn't telling me if I got it right?"

There's a loud groan from the mummified knight in the wheelchair.

Judge Wolf sighs and rolls his eyes to the ceiling.

Uncle Jasper ignores Dash's question. "Officer Dash, the photos showed the face of the dragons, but you couldn't see Horace's face clearly from such a distance. So, how did you know it was Horace at the accident?"

The knight laughs. "Oh! Now I see what you're doing. The victim told me."

Another loud groan comes from under the bandages of the victim., Sir Little.

"Ah. It was the victim who told you it was the defendant and not just any other dragon."

"Sure, Sir Little described him to me."

"And you wrote it down on the accident report?"

"Yup. I always do."

Emily writes the word "smug" on her pad and tilts it toward me.

I scribble back, "Agree. He thinks he's past the worst."

Uncle Jasper walks back to the table and picks up a copy of the accident report. "Would you please read me lines 7-9 of your report?"

The knight reads: "Upon arriving at the scene of the accident, I saw a dragon flying away and a knight lying on the ground with extensive injuries."

"Did you write that?" Uncle Jasper asks.

"Of course."

"Read two lines lower, please?"

The witness finds the lines and reads: "The knight's helmet was shoved sideways, visor damaged and locked closed, and he was moaning loudly, as if in terrible pain. He kept crying out that he couldn't feel his legs and arms and couldn't...see..."

"He couldn't what?"

The officer's gulp is heard throughout the courtroom. "Well, he said, he couldn't see. Yeah, but that was maybe because his helmet was closed. It was badly damaged. I couldn't open it." Dash squirms in his seat, but quickly recovers and says, "He isn't blind now, is he? That just shows how hard the dragon hit him! He caused a lot of damage."

Judge Wolf stares at Sir Little. "Are you blind, Sir Little?"

Sir Little replies in a low, low voice. "No, but...but...when the officer came to me, I was so badly hurt that I couldn't see."

"So, you couldn't really see who knocked you off your horse?" Uncle Jasper is in front of Sir Little.

"It was that dragon! It was him! He tried to kill me! He plowed right into me!"

"But you couldn't see him. Even if you weren't blind, your friend here said your helmet was turned the wrong way, and your visor was locked down, so how could you identify Horace as your alleged attacker?"

Officer Dash interrupts, "He saw him before the accident. How can you miss a dragon?"

A few knights laugh, but most are silent.

Uncle Jasper turns back to Dash. "That makes sense."

Dash smiles, confident again. "Of course, it does. You gotta know when a dragon crashes into you. It's not like a tiny mouse bumping into you. Right? Right?"

"So, your friend saw the defendant before the crash happened, well enough to describe him to you?"

Dash clears his throat. "He's not my friend, but yes, that's how it happened."

"But he couldn't avoid the crash after seeing this gigantic dragon coming at him?"

"I...guess not. I mean, how do you avoid a big thing charging right at you?"

"You're an expert witness. As an expert, would you say if Sir Little hadn't been drinking three beers at the Dead Dragon Inn that might have helped him avoid the accident?"

"No. I mean, it's hard to avoid a dragon racing at you at high speed."

"But as an expert witness, would you agree that drinking three beers might slow down your reaction time?"

The officer looks flustered. "I suppose. Maybe a little."

"Contributory negligence," I write on the pad and slide it over to Emily. She nods and writes. "At least we got that."

"So, your friend could have avoided the accident if—"

"I keep telling you, he's not my friend! I hardly know him!" Dash shouts.

Uncle Jasper looks apologetic. "I'm sorry. I just naturally thought you and Sir Little are friends...both of you being knights. My mistake, I guess."

Dash laughs. "Do you think every knight knows every other knight in the whole world? You're a knight, and I'm definitely not your friend." He laughs again. "None of us are."

Some of the knights in the gallery laugh. Most look angry.

"You're right. I am a knight. I'm just not your kind of knight," Uncle Jasper says.

One glance at the gallery, and I can see that some of the knights are also definitely not my uncle's friends either. They look like they'd like to get him into a dark alley and tear him apart. I don't like these guys. I know some of them are Dragonslayers. It's like they belong to a secret club, and if one of them does something wrong, they have to support him. It's as if they don't have a brain of their own, but follow their leader, even if he's doing something bad. In school, a few kids started a club like that. They swore an oath to keep it secret. To get in, you had to punch another kid. I wanted to join that club so bad but couldn't punch an innocent kid. I knew that was wrong. These guys have to kill dragons....

My uncle could never kill a dragon. I look at Robin and know he's not like the others. He'd never hurt Horace. Or would he? Is he in on it too?

CHAPTER 28

Uncle Jasper is back at our table. "Are you okay, Brodie?"

"Are you really a knight? Are you a Dragonslayer?" I whisper, sure he would never join that secret club.

Uncle Jasper looks surprised and then shakes his head. "Of course not. You should know better." He shakes his head again. "Now, let me get back to work?" He heads to the front of the courtroom. "Miss Beanstalk, would you mind standing for a moment?" Uncle Jasper nods in her direction.

Emily stands. For once, she looks a little nervous.

"Officer Dash, do you know my assistant, Miss Emily Beanstalk?"

"No. I never saw the young lady before."

"Miss Beanstalk, would you please tell the court where you were today?"

"I was retrieving files from the Monstrovian Police Records room."

Judge Wolf grunts. "Excuse me, Mr. Goode, why aren't you objecting to this line of questioning?"

"Your honor, to save time, the prosecution will agree that the records collected by Mr. Doofinch's assistants are genuine and may be used as evidence in this trial."

"Are you sure?" Judge Wolf asks.

Goode nods. "Absolutely."

"Very well, continue, Mr. Doofinch."

Uncle Jasper smiles a thank you to Goode. "You may be seated, Miss Beanstalk. Thank you."

Emily sits. She looks a little shaky.

Being a witness in court can do that to you. "You did good," I say.

She gives me a smile and looks straight ahead.

Uncle Jasper holds up a sheet of paper. "You say you're not friends with the victim, is that right?"

"I already told you."

Uncle Jasper looks at the paper and then looks at the witness with a confused expression on his face. "I don't understand something then."

"You don't understand a lot of things," Dash says and laughs.

A few knights laugh, but most are watching silently.

Uncle Jasper smiles. "Very good. My other assistant found it kind of curious and brought it to my attention." He hands the witness the thick file. "This is a directory of accident cases filed by your police precinct over the last five years." He holds up another sheet of paper. "Miss Beanstalk went through every single case, and guess what she found?"

"I have no idea."

"Well, look at case 3 and then look at case 273. Notice anything unusual?"

"No. This is a waste of time." He looks at Goode, but the lawyer is silent.

Uncle Jasper shrugs his shoulders. "Nothing? Okay. The two cases are exactly the same."

"So, what? There are thousands of cases in this file. It's just a coincidence."

"You may be right. But my nephew looked for more cases with your name on them, and there weren't any. For years, there were accident cases with your name as the reporting officer, and then none. Brodie thought that was strange."

"What's strange? I was assigned to other work. I don't do accidents that much anymore. Nothing strange about that."

"You're right again. But Brodie noticed something else. Take a look at the signature line for this report. Would you read it aloud?"

"It's my name. No big deal."

"I said, please read it aloud?"

Dash shakes his head. "This is a waste of time."

"Please, read it aloud?" Judge Wolf says, his eyes showing he means business.

The officer shakes his head and reads, "B. Alder Dash."

"That's not exactly what it says."

"It's my initials. So, what?"

"So, suddenly, five years ago, you went from signing accident reports with your full name to just using your initials."

"I don't understand why you're making such a big deal out of this. I still use my full name for my criminal cases and B.A.D. for others. No mystery there."

Judge Wolf shakes his head. "I don't understand why you're doing this either," he says.

"I think Officer Dash knows very well why this is important."

"I have no idea." Dash looks at Goode.

"I had my assistant, Miss Beanstalk, go through the files again. Based on a hunch by my nephew, I asked her to list every case signed with only your initials."

"Now that's a real waste of time," Dash says. "This is too. I don't see what you're trying to prove."

"Brodie, how many cases did you find with the officer's initials, B.A.D., only?"

I stand up. "Seventeen. I found seventeen cases with only the initials."

"See. Hardly any. It's just a coincidence."

"Emily, when you cross-referenced those cases, did you find anything unusual?"

Emily stands. "At first no, but then I read through all the boring stuff—and it was really boring—"

"And what did you find out?"

The officer shouts, "Hey, Goode, what kinda' lawyer are you? Aren't you going to object to this?"

Goode shakes his head. "You deserve what you get."

Dash jumps from his seat and leaps over the witness box railing. He shouts at the gallery, "Kill them! Brothers, kill them!"

Goode shoots out his arm and knocks Dash onto the floor.

The knights in the gallery are on their feet.

Robin Hood holds up his hands. "Sit down, gentlemen. It's time you learn the truth."

Two bear-heads lift the dazed officer from the floor and hold him up facing the judge.

"Now, where do you think you're going?" Judge Wolf says. "Return him to the witness stand and keep guard. If he moves again, he'll be in irons." He glares at the knights. "And you, sit down now, or I'll have your whole secret club locked up." He looks at me and grunts, "They hunt wolves too."

The guards place Dash back on the chair. He shakes his head to clear it.

Uncle Jasper glances at Dash and abruptly turns to Sir Little. "You know why he ran, don't you, Sir Little?"

A low whining noise comes from under the bandages.

"Miss Beanstalk, what did you discover when you checked all those boring papers that nobody ever looks through?"

Emily smiles. "The victims in all seventeen accidents were…"

There's a sudden noise.

I look at the bandaged knight. Sir Little is on his feet and clumping clumsily, as fast as he can scramble in all those bandages, toward the exit.

A blur of green jumps from the gallery and lands in front of the door. "And just where are you going, Sir Little?" Robin asks, gripping the 'mummy' by his arm. "You move fast for a grievously injured accident victim." He hands the knight to two waiting guards who drag him to a chair at the front of the room.

Goode stands. "Your honor, I swear I did not know about any of this."

Judge Wolf holds his gavel high in the air, his eyes glaring at Goode. "If at proving your innocence, you do fail, Mr. Goode, you'll spend your life in jail."

Uncle Jasper shakes his head. "Your honor, I assure you Mr. Goode had absolutely no idea of what was going on until I told him what my nephew discovered last night. Once my colleague saw the proof, he was totally cooperative. It was these two Dragonslayers who cooked up this devious scheme. Goode is a good man and a good lawyer."

Wolf sits down. "Very well, I'll accept he didn't know about this somehow. Let's learn who's behind this mess right now!"

Uncle Jasper studies the two knights and then walks to the dazed Officer Dash. "You almost got away with it. You're facing a lifetime in prison. Do you know what happens to police when they are in prison with criminals—"

Sir Little cries out, "I told him it wouldn't work. I told him if we kept doing it, we'd get caught. One was fine. Two, we could get away with. But he wouldn't stop."

Uncle Jasper rushes toward the bandaged knight. "Who did you tell? Whose idea was it for you to fake your accidents?"

A loud scream comes from Officer Dash, "He's lying! It was him! It was all his idea!"

"No. It was Baldric's scheme! He swore we'd never get caught. Nobody would care if a dragon got punished. We'd make a lot of money from the insurance company, and the dragon would be out of the picture, dead from resisting arrest or rotting in prison!"

Dash screams, "You liar! You set this whole thing up, and now you're blaming me!"

"You jerk! You picked on Doofinch's dragon?"

"Shut up both of you," Judge Wolf blasts at them. "Guards, take them far away from me! Lock them up and throw away the key."

The bear-heads grab Officer Dash from the stand and drag him toward the side door. "Doofinch, please help me? It was Little. He's framing me! I'll pay you to defend me! I have money! Lots of money! Please? I need a good lawyer."

The knight in bandages is being carried through the courtroom. "Doofinch, don't listen to him. I'll pay you more if you defend me? We're both knights! He's a rat in knight's clothes. I'm your brother! I'm your brother!"

"You're no brother of mine." Uncle Jasper watches in disgust as the two are taken from the courtroom.

I feel so relieved. "I can't believe it's over.

Uncle Jasper smiles at Emily and me. "You both did good work. Excellent, in fact." He looks at me. "Brodie, I know you don't love paperwork, but this case should show you how important it is to read everything having to do with a trial very, very carefully. If you hadn't found those records—"

"Uncle, I have to tell you, it was Silas who found the first clue."

"Really? Silas? Our Silas? Well, I guess those glassed helped him after all."

He places his arm around my shoulder. "Let's go home."

I'm about to help him pack his stuff when I notice Judge Wolf staring at Horace still in the cage. "Uncle Jasper, why isn't Horace free yet?"

The Judge looks down at me. "Son, I can answer that. Even though those two criminals seem to have worked together to fake this accident, the law says they're innocent until they stand trial."

Emily sags into her seat. "I thought proving they set this whole thing up and did it a bunch of times, would be all we'd need. Poor Horace."

Uncle Jasper sighs. "The judge is right. Those two haven't been put on trial, so they're considered innocent, and we have to finish this."

The judge nods. "While it certainly appears that those two deliberately caused the accident and that Sir Lance A. Little faked his injuries, there is still the question of Horace leaving the scene. That is a serious crime, and so far, there is nothing that shows he didn't do that. Am I correct, Mr. Goode?"

Goode has been silent. I realize he helped my uncle catch the bad guys, but still don't like, or trust him. He stands and faces Judge Wolf. "Your honor, you're right. In fact, we have several other witnesses who will testify they saw a dragon answering the defendant's description flying away from the scene. Their descriptions match the defendant perfectly."

Emily pokes my arm with her nails.

Poor Horace. Uncle Jasper and Goode may have made a deal to trap the two baddies, but the District Attorney isn't going to drop the charge of hit-and-run, the most serious crime in this case. To him, it's still a contest, and he wants to win. "Uncle, can't you do anything?"

"I wish I could. All we can do is question the witnesses and hope we can add doubt. But I read the reports. I think their stories will stick. Horace did run away from the accident scene before help arrived."

"Maybe he was frightened?" Emily repeats what I said when the case began.

"No excuse, Emily. Nobody should ever leave an accident scene until help arrives." I get no pleasure, for once, showing off what I learned.

Uncle Jasper nods. "The only one who knows what really happened, Sir Little, is in jail. I doubt if he'd talk anyway, not without a deal."

Goode looks at his file and then says, "Call…call…Sheriff Hood…No. Call

Brodie Adkins to the stand."

"Me?" And I thought this couldn't get worse?

CHAPTER 29

"What?" Uncle Jasper asks, a frightened look on his face.

"What?" Emily asks, digging her nails into my arm.

"Ouch! Emily!" I shout. "Who me?"

Judge Wolf looks at Goode. "You're calling Mr. Doofinch's assistant...er...nephew?"

"Please, your honor," Goode says.

I look at my uncle for help, but he seems stunned. I stand up, straighten my jacket, wish I wasn't wearing sneakers, and walk to the witness stand. My legs feel like jello. I take the oath and settle uneasily onto the witness chair. My feet don't even reach the floor. I'm a nervous wreck.

"Brodie, may I call you that?"

Goode is like a building standing in front of me. I can't see my uncle. I'd even settle on seeing Emily. "Yes. I guess so." I hate this guy. He turned on my uncle after making it look like they were on the same side.

"You don't like me, do you?"

"What does that have to do...No, I guess not."

"Why is that?"

"Objection!" Uncle Jasper shouts. "This has nothing to do with the case. I don't know what you want from my nephew at all?"

"It appears to me, I must agree," Judge Wolf says.

"Please, your honor?" He waits for the judge's approval and continues, "But you do like Horace? Why is that? He's a dragon. Everybody knows they're violent and eat anything, or anyone, that gets in their way."

Uncle Jasper looks like a spring about to pop up again, but stops in midleap."

I pause to think about my answer. "I used to think that dragons were no good too. Before I came to Monstrovia and learned from my uncle, I hated dragons. That's the way I was taught." I look at Horace and wish I knew how much he understands of what I'm saying. "I guess there are bad dragons, but there are also good ones...bad lawyers, but good ones too."

"And Horace is?"

Whose side is Goode on? "Horace is a good one, Mr. Goode, a really good one."

"How do you know? How do you know he's a good one?"

"He saved my life a couple times. He risked his own life and saved me...and Emily. Yup, he's a good one." I look at Horace and wonder if he's smiling.

"Isn't it true he broke the law when he flew after he lost his license?"

Again, Uncle Jasper looks ready to attack but stays in his seat, scowling at Goode.

"Horace lost his license because some people thought he was too old to fly. Uncle Jasper proved that age shouldn't automatically stop anyone from doing anything. But even so, Horace only flew because it was the only way he could save Emily and me. He would never have broken the law—"

"You like him, don't you?"

"I love him."

"And you like your uncle."

I look at Uncle Jasper. *Why isn't he objecting?* "Yes. I like him...I love him."

Uncle Jasper is back in his chair. He always tries not to show emotions during a trial, but he looks emotional right now.

Goode nods. "I've had my staff do some research about you."

I freeze. *What does Goode mean by that?*

He opens a folder. "It says you got in quite a bit of trouble with your school, a number of times. Is that true?"

"Objection. My nephew isn't on trial here."

"Objection sustained. Goode, I'm stewing. What are you doing?"

"One minute more, your honor. I promise you'll see the connection soon." Goode scans the file. "Brodie, why is it you got in trouble at your old home,

120

but here your record is spotless?"

I'm so angry I can hardly speak. I really feel like I'm on trial. Emily's eyes are burning me up. "My uncle helped me."

Goode is silent.

What's he waiting for, the snake?

The silence makes me uneasy. "My uncle is the greatest man I know. He makes sure I don't do anything stupid. He says if I want to be a lawyer or anything good in life, I have to do what's right."

Goode nods. "So, your uncle takes good care of you and makes sure you do the right things. And you still love him?"

I smile at my uncle. "Yes. Yes, I do."

Goode turns to Judge Wolf. "Your honor, based on Brodie's testimony, I believe that Mr. Doofinch, my colleague, is an excellent caregiver. He has the rare ability to make certain those in his charge learn right from wrong, and still love him. He has done a wonderful job with his nephew, turning a child who seemed destined for trouble—even throwing mudballs at his principal's car—yes, we know about that, Mr. Adkins." He gives me a smile. "As I said, turning a child headed for trouble, perhaps even becoming a law-breaker, into someone we all can be proud of." He smiles at me again.

I'm not sure how I feel about what he's saying. I'm nervous and embarrassed but also surprised. Is this really Goode?

"Your honor, the state does not want revenge, but that a person learns to do what is right. In this case, the defendant broke an important law. Whatever the reason, leaving the accident victim was still a serious crime. But if Mr. Doofinch can guide this boy to success, I believe he can 'train' this dragon to do what is right." He smiles at my uncle. "Your honor, the state will drop all charges under the condition that Mr. Doofinch accepts responsibility for Horace for no less than two years and promises to teach him never to leave the scene of an accident again."

Uncle Jasper is out of his seat like a rocket. "Of course, I will." He rushes toward Goode, his hand extended. "Thank you, Hugh. Thank you."

I'm speechless. Is this the Goode I hated? It must be a trick.

Uncle Jasper pulls me gently from the witness chair. "Brodie, it's over. My boy, you did it again."

Judge Wolf bangs his gavel. "Order! Order! Everyone take your seats! Oh, no. This isn't over until I say so!"

Uncle Jasper mutters, "He's right. He can still mess things up."

Emily whispers in my ear, "You were amazing."

"Thank you." Maybe Emily's not so bad.

Judge Wolf glares at Goode. "Mr. Goode, did I hear, right? You're dropping all charges?"

Even Goode sounds frightened. "Yes, your honor. In the state's opinion, the best way to serve justice is to return the defendant to the family that loves him."

I can't believe Goode's saying that. I've hated him ever since our first case. Was I wrong?

Judge Wolf's eyes are red. They look like flames are in their center.

"He scares me when he looks like that," I whisper to Emily.

She holds my hand.

I let her but pull it under the table.

Uncle Jasper looks like he's stopped breathing, his eyes riveted on the judge.

Judge Wolf snarls, "You're all in for a big surprise. Will the defendant rise?"

Oh boy! He's rhyming.

Uncle Jasper stands. Emily and I stand. Horace is still in the cage, but his neck is fully extended, eyes on the judge.

Judge Wolf picks up his gavel. "In all my years as a lawyer, and now as a judge, I've never heard of a case—"

I can't breathe. What's Wolf going to do? He's the judge. He can mess everything up!

Judge Wolf opens his mouth. His teeth are sharp and white against his black fur. "I've never heard of a case where two lawyers..." He looks at me. "Where two lawyers love justice so much that they're willing to forget their differences and do what is best for everyone involved." He slams the gavel on his table and exclaims, "Case dismissed. The defendant is freed in the custody of Jasper Doofinch and his nephew. I'm proud of all of you."

I run over to where Horace is still looking frightened in his cage. "It's okay, boy. You're free. You're coming home with me."

A bear-head unlocks the cage. Another pulls open the steel gate.

Uncle Jasper coaxes Horace, who looks confused and frightened, from the cage. "Come on, Horace, old man, we're going home."

I reach up and run my hand down his massive neck.

Emily strokes his neck too.

I guess if he likes her, she can't be all that bad.

"May I pet him?"

Shock of shocks, it's Goode! For once, he doesn't look like a shark or a bully, but frightened, like I was before I got to know Horace.

"Sure," I say, and guide his hand to just under Horace's chin. Suddenly, I remember there's someone I want to thank. I search the courtroom, but Robin Hood is gone. I wonder if we'll ever see him again.

THE END

More from Monstrovia

Thank you for helping solve this case. We hope you enjoyed it and want to read more in this multi-award-winning series:

Book 1: WELCOME TO MONSTROVIA: What would you do if you found yourself trapped with a strange uncle in a land where humans are rare? Would you run away or stay to help solve a murder with a hilarious surprise ending? Silver Medal, Benjamin Franklyn Book Awards/First Prize Unpublished Middle-Grade Fiction, Florida Writers Association/Bronze Medal, Readers Favorite Awards.

Book 2: THE CASE OF THE DISASTROUS DRAGON: Life is one disaster after another when Brodie, Jasper, and Emily must try and save a fire-breathing dragon from prison. 2nd Place, Florida Writers Association/A Top Ten Children's Book, P&E Readers Poll.

Book 3: THE CASE OF THE CRAZY CHICKENSCRATCHES: Is he crazy, or is there a secret behind his strange behavior? All his neighbors want to kill him and only Jasper, Brodie and Emily can solve the mystery, but Brodie has a big problem of his own to solve that could change everything.

COMING SOON! Book 5: THE CASE OF THE FIRE-BREATHING FIREFIGHTER: Brodie, Jasper, and Emily must learn the secret of the Dragonslayer Knights to learn why a fire-breathing dragon started a ferocious forest fire in book 5 of this multi-award-winning mystery series that introduces law with fantasy cases.

YOUR KIND REVIEWS ON AMAZON AND GOODREADS ARE SIN-
CERELY APPRECIATED.

THANK YOU,

BRODIE AND MARK

Visit www.aimhipress.com for all our great books, news, contests, and
freebies.

Visit AimHiPress.com for more books and other products from AimHi Press and the rest of the Newhouse Creative Group family!

Newhouse Creative Group: Inspiring the Readers and Writers of Today and Tomorrow

Also by Mark H. Newhouse

Mark's books have won awards from Readers Favorite, The Benjamin Franklin Book Awards, The Florida Writers Association, and many others. He welcomes your comments, kind support, and reviews.

The Rockhound Science Mysteries (English Bilingual)
Teachers' Choice Award- Learning Magazine
Children love solving funny mysteries with experiments such as making ice pops.

Alice in Batsylvania
Readers Choice 5 Star Award
Alice, warned not to go off with strangers, doesn't listen. Animated illustrations make this fun picture book with a twist ending leap to life.

Santa's Speeding Ticket
Officer Zapper is almost run down by an unusual speeder. Funny illustrations and surprise make this a holiday treasure.

The Devil's Bookkeepers: Books 1 and 2
"What Anne Frank did for Dutch Jews, The Devil's Bookkeepers does for the Jews of the Lodz ghetto."
A suspenseful novel of love and courage as a group of men and their controversial leader struggle to save themselves and their loved ones during the Holocaust.
5 Stars- Readers' Favorite

About the Author

Mark is a multi-award-winning author of books for children and adults. Born in Germany to Holocaust survivors, his novels set in the ghetto his parents were among the few to miraculously survive, The Devil's Bookkeepers, won the Gold Medal Historical Fiction and top honor of Best Book of the Year from the Florida Writers Association. An intense story of love, friendship, and painful decisions in a time of terror, the characters face incredible situations and gripping suspense as they struggle to deal with the tightening Nazi noose.

Other award-winning books include Welcome to Monstrovia, The Case of the Disastrous Dragon, The Case of the Crazy Chickenscratches, The Rockhound Science Mysteries, and more. His picture books include Alice in Batsylvania; A Bite Before Christmas; Santa's Speeding Ticket; Dreidel Dog; and the Passover Puppy Coloring Book. A retired Long Island teacher, he now lives in Florida, with his wife, and is the state Chairperson of the Florida Writers Association Youth Program and a member of FWA's Board of Directors. Founding president of Writers League (www.wlov.org), he is the founder/leader of Writers 4 Kids. He also writes the monthly Writing Bug column for Village Neighbors Magazine. He can be reached at www.newhousecreativegroup.com

"Thank you, readers, for your kind support and reviews."

www.ingramcontent.com/pod-product-compliance
Lightning Source LLC
Chambersburg PA
CBHW071359170626
46811CB00003B/1178